# Judgment Day

# Judgment Day

## Anya Nicole

www.urbanbooks.net

Urban Books, LLC
78 East Industry Court
Deer Park, NY 11729

ISBN 13: 978-1-60162-272-3
ISBN 10: 1-60162-272-4

First Printing June 2010
Printed in the United States of America

10 9 8 7 6 5 4 3 2 1

Distributed by Kensington Publishing Corp.
Submit Wholesale Orders to:
Kensington Publishing Corp.
C/O Penguin Group (USA) Inc.
Attention: Order Processing
405 Murray Hill Parkway
East Rutherford, NJ 07073-2316
Phone: 1-800-526-0275
Fax: 1-800-227-9604

# Dedication

This book is dedicated to my husband and daughter. It's nothing else in the world more important to me than my family.

# Acknowledgments

Wow! Book number two! Just a year and a half ago this was all a dream. I continue to thank God for giving me the strength to move forward in life, and I will continue to praise Him. I want to thank all the readers who supported *Corporate Corner Boyz* and are anxiously awaiting the sequel.

To my mother Jacqueline: Ever since you left me I've been lost. I pray every day and I ask God to give me the strength you raised me to have during these trying times. What hurts me the most is knowing that you will never meet your granddaughter.

To my husband Termayne: You are my strength, and I thank you for hustling hard to make my dream a reality. To my daughter Sydney, you are the reason I get up in the morning, and I want you to know that everything I do, I do with you in mind. Always remember that Mommy loves you, no matter what.

Shalena, thanks for being such a good friend and helping me through my trials and tribulations. Also, thanks for editing my work before I turned it in.

Wavey, thank you for your advice, encouragement, and being available to listen to my crazy rants. Iris, thanks for continuing to support my dream and being there also when I need to talk. I'm grateful to be surrounded by such brilliant people.

To Anna J., thank you for being such a good friend outside

# Acknowledgments

the book game; you were ready to go to war for a sista, and I will never forget it. To Nakea S. Murray, thank you for your advice, patience, and encouragement during this crazy ride.

To the Queens by Birthright Book Club: No one throws a party like you do!

Thanks for having me, Mrs. Sharon. You are that girl!

To Karen Johnson, thanks for supporting my project and continuing to spread the word about *Corporate Corner Boyz* and hopefully *Judgment Day*.

To Mona, babe, you will always be the best makeup artist known to woman. To Terry Lewis Photography, I trust no one else with my photos. Big Bro STYLIST, thanks for continuing to support me also.

To Margaret, thanks for being my longtime friend, my best friend and helping me transform into the woman I am today.

To The "Real Dudes," I still think you all are some of the best dudes on the planet. Thanks for being there for me when it seemed as though the walls were closing in on me.

As I write these acknowledgments, I come to you with a heavy heart. On September 16th, 2008, my brother-in-law was brutally murdered in the streets of Philadelphia. When someone close to you is taken away, it really makes you look at the world differently. You never think it's going to happen to your family, and when it does you're in disbelief. Rest in Peace, Roc. God knows better than all of us.

I promise to keep bringing the heat as long as you continue reading. I love writing as much as I love my family; it's one of the most important things in my life.

Much love,
Anya Nicole

# Friend or Foe

Chris flipped through the paper and there was a picture of himself and Brandon popping champagne at the label's launch party over a year and a half ago. *He couldn't have sold the label without me*, Chris thought. *We had equal ownership rights.* Chris wanted to call their lawyer, but it was too early. He sat on the edge of the rickety full-size motel bed and watched the clock almost two hours until it reached nine A.M. These were the longest two hours of his life. He picked up his cell phone and dialed the lawyer as soon as the second hand on the clock reached twelve.

"Good morning. Richardson Entertainment Law Group," the receptionist answered in a delightful tone.

"Let me speak to Attorney Richardson," Chris growled into the phone.

"I'm sorry, but he's just getting in. May I take a message?" she asked.

"Bitch, just put him on the phone!" Chris yelled, jumping up from the bed and pacing back and forth.

She covered the phone to speak to someone, and Attorney Richardson picked up the line.

"Yes, this is Attorney Richardson. Can I help you?" he asked, somewhat annoyed that he was being called to the phone before he had his morning coffee.

"How did Brandon sell the label without me?"

Attorney Richardson took a deep breath and then began to speak. "You signed over your rights, Chris. You don't remember?"

Chris became quiet. The lawyer must have been talking about the papers he'd signed a while back when the law was on his heels. Chris hung up the phone and sat back down on the bed.

*Brandon must have planned this all along,* Chris thought. He'd pressured Chris to sign those papers, and Chris was too busy to read them through. He figured he didn't have to because he and Brandon were like brothers, and Brandon would always have his best interest at heart.

Chris wanted his half of the money. Brandon had him hot under the collar, talking to him like he was some big-shot nigga. He didn't run shit. Chris was the one who put Brandon on.

When Brandon's mother died, it was Chris and his mother Ms. Ruth who accepted into their family. *Ungrateful bastard.* Brandon was getting way out if line, and Chris was ready to put him back in check.

It was time for Chris to show his face around the projects again. He'd been hiding for a month. The cops were probably still searching for him, but he had to make some serious moves. He had never gotten another hammer, and he needed one now more than ever. He had a hunch that things were going to get ugly between him and Brandon. He wanted his share, and he was going to come for it full force. As far as he was concerned, Brandon was just another the nigga from off the street that needed to get dealt with. *Besides it ain't like I don't deserve my cut.* Chris had worked hard finding artists and putting all of his money into Brandon's dream.

Plus, if he was to avoid doing time, he needed to hire a

top-notch attorney who knew his shit, and that wasn't gonna come cheap.

He put his hood on his head as he left the hotel, got in his car, and drove toward North Philly. As soon as he crossed the Girard Avenue Bridge, his blood started to rush. He was home and ready to get shit poppin'.

It was still early when he got to the projects, so not many people were out. Still, he circled the block three times before he parked, and then he got out of the car and went straight into the building.

The guard was too busy running his mouth on his cell phone to even see Chris pass by. Chris got on the elevator and made his way up to Tank's crib. He was going to get the rest of his clothes while he was there.

He opened the door to Tank's bedroom and walked in on some fine-ass redbone giving Tank some head. Chris walked right past the bed and grabbed his bags from the closet. Tank was too tied up to say a word, so Chris opened up every one of Tank's dresser drawers until he found a gun. Ever since he had known Tank he'd always kept his money and drugs in one drawer, and guns in another. He quickly stuffed the gun in his bag and rolled out.

As Chris approached his car he noticed a piece of pipe lying in the grass. He grabbed it and put it in the backseat with the rest of his things, figuring it couldn't hurt to have an extra weapon.

Next Chris drove over to the parking lot of Mia's building to shake Brandon up a littlebit, and cause a little confusion in the process. He rode up beside Brandon's jeep and got out the car. Grabbing the pipe from the backseat, he used it to bust Brandon's front windshield, and then he took his keys and keyed the side of Brandon's car.

The car alarm was going off, but Chris needed to add a

finishing touch, so he quickly ran over to the passenger's side of his own car. He pulled out a switchblade from the glove compartment and used it to flatten every tire on the jeep. Once Brandon's car was totally vandalized, Chris got back in his own car and pulled off.

Chris smiled to himself. Not only did he just fuck up Brandon's main mode of transportation, but he made it look like a bitch did it, to stir up trouble on the home front. Chris wanted to hang around in the cut to see the expression on Brandon's and Mia's faces when they saw the jeep, so he parked two rows over and waited.

The alarm sounded for a good twenty minutes before the building personnel notified Brandon.

As the phone rang inside the apartment, Mia looked over at Brandon, hoping he would answer, but he was sound asleep. She reached over him and grabbed the phone off the receiver.

"Hello."

"Mrs. Brunson, the alarm on your husband's jeep is going off. It seems that someone has vandalized it," the front desk agent reported. "Please report to the parking lot. The authorities are on their way."

Mia threw the receiver on the floor and scrambled to her feet.

"Wake up! Wake up!" she shouted at Brandon.

Brandon sat up, looked around, and wiped the slobber off the side of his mouth.

"What's wrong?" he asked.

"Someone broke into your car," shae said as she slipped on her slippers and tied her robe.

Brandon put on his slippers, grabbed his keys, and headed to the elevators. Mia locked the door behind them. A police officer was already on the scene by the time they got down to the parking gargage. Brandon's face wrinkled up as soon as he saw the car.

Chris watched as Brandon threw his hands up in the air. *This is only the beginning*, Chris thought.

"What the fuck!" Brandon blurted out as he observed the damage.

The car was so fucked up that Brandon wanted to trade it in as soon as he saw the smashed front winsheild. He turned and looked at Mia. She was standing there tapping her foot as if she was about to have a fit. He knew that she probably thought Lynn had done this, but Brandon didn't think so. Brandon finished making the report with the police officer, and then walked back over to Mia.

As the officer pulled off , Chris could tell that Brandon and Mia were arguing. She was pointing her finger in Brandon's face.

Chris was making Brandon's life miserable and enjoying it. Yet it wasn't enough. He wanted Brandon to know that it was him. He turned the car on as Mia and Brandon walked back to the elevators.

"I know it was her," Mia said. "I knew she was going to do something like this."

*Mia has it all wrong*, Brandon thought. This wasn't even Lynn's style. He knew Mia was never going to forgive him.

"It wasn't her," Brandon said.

"So who was it?" she asked. " Some other bitch that yu forgot to tell me vabout?"

Chris rode past slowly, rolled down the window, and smiled. Mia was too busy chewing out Brandon's ass to notice the car slowly riding by.

Brandon grew angry as soon as he realized it was Chris.

"Did you see that?" Brandon yelled to Mia.

"See what?" she asked.

He grabbed her hand and hurried to the elevators. When they got back to the apartment Brandon put on a pair of sweatpants and a gray thermal shirt. He slipped on a fresh pair of Timbs and went into the bathroom to brush his teeth.

Mia stood in the doorway of the bathroom and watched while he gargled.

"Where are you going?" she asked.

He finished up and wiped his mouth with a hand towel. "I gotta go out for a few. I'll be back a little later," he said.

By now Mia had grown suspicious. He could be going to see another woman.

"Why can't you tell me where you're going?"

He grabbed her shoulders, turned her around, and led her to the bedroom.

"Look, I have to go handle something with Chris," he said.

Mia's stomach instantly dropped.

"Do me a favor and stay in the house , OK? At least until I get back home. If anything strange happens, call the police."

After Mia agreed to stay inside, Brandon grabbed his Sean John coat and left. He had no means of transportation, so he dialed Lynn's cell phone.

"Hello." She sounded as if the phone had interrupted her sleep.

"Hey, it's me. I need you to pick me up," he said.

"When?"

"Right now! My car is fucked up, and I need to use yours."

"Where are you?" she asked.

While Brandon walked and talked, he kept glancing over his shoulder to make sure he wasn't being followed.

"Meet me on the corner of Nineteenth and Market, in front of the bank."

"OK, OK, I'll be there," Lynn said as she dragged herself out of bed.

Brandon waited by the entrance to the bank. He watched everyone who passed him, making sure Chris didn't walk up on him.

Lynn honked the horn, and Brandon got in the car. She drove back to her apartment, got out of the car, and left the keys with Brandon.

Brandon knew Chris was a dirty-ass nigga, but he never thought he would stoop that low. Leave it to Chris to do some fag shit and key his car. Only bitches did shit like that. Brandon knew he needed to buy a gun, because he knew Chris wouldn't let up until he got what he wanted.

When Chris and Brandon were little, Chris had to win at everything or he started a fight. Brandon remembered the time when Chris lost a basketball game in summer camp when they were about sixteen years old. Chris missed the last shot and was so mad that he punched the ref in the mouth. He was a hot-headed nigga, and Brandon was going to have to cool him off.

The only person Brandon knew in the hood who sold guns was Tank. He knew Tank was Chris's man, but he also knew Tank was about his business. If you needed it, he had it, and he didn't care what you did with it, as long as you didn't mention his name when you got caught.

Brandon was sure that he would find Tank in front of the Dominican store. He always saw him there when he used to drop off Chris at the projects.

He pulled around the side of the store and parked. Peeping around the corner, he waved for Tank to come over.

Tank looked around and then pointed to himself. "Who, me?"

"Yeah, you," Brandon said.

Tank pulled up his pants as he walked around to the side of the store. Once he got closer he started to smile when he figured out who Brandon was.

"Oh, shit, it's the uppity nigga who thinks he's from the suburbs," Tank said. He looked Brandon up and down. "What you need?" Tank already had an idea about what was going on. In fact, the whole hood knew Brandon had sold out Chris., Brandon looked Tank in the eyes.

"I need a gun."

Tank laughed. He pulled out a dime bag of weed and a blunt. "So what kind you looking for?" He continued to roll up while he waited for Brandon to answer.

"I don't know. Nigga, just give me what you got," Brandon said. He looked around to see who was watching. There was no one around, but Brandon was a bit paranoid. He had never purchased a gun before, and he had no clue what kind of gun he needed. He just wanted to make sure he could protect himself and his wife if Chris came after them.

Thank shook his head. *This nigga is about to go to war with a veteran in the game and he don't even know what kind of gun he needs,* Tank thought.

Brandon leaned on the car while Tank disappeared into the alley a little farther down the street. He returned with a brown paper bag.

"How much you tryin' to spend?" Tank asked.

"Whatever, " Brandon said.

"Give me five hundred," Tank said. "I charge extra for uppity niggas."

Brandon got back in the car and counted his money. He had taken a grand out of the bank while he was waiting for Lynn to pick him up.

"It's all there," Brandon said as he watched Tank count out the money. When Tank finished, he handed Brandon the brown paper bag and walked off.

Brandon got back in the car, drove up a block, and parked. The bag felt kind of light, so he wanted to make sure Tank ain't gagged him. He opened the bag and took out the gun. It was a baby .22 with a pearl handle.

This is a bitch's gun, Brandon thought. It was so small, a chick could put it in her purse and no one would ever know. But it would have to do for now.

Brandon drove back to the apartment. When he got there Mia was in the kitchen cooking. There was smoke in the hallway, so she must have burned something, as usual.

Brandon came in and grabbed a beer from the fridge. He could tell by the look on Mia's face that she was annoyed. She looked at him and continued flouring chicken. Brandon got a glimpse of the meal and lost his appetite. He could tell Mia had never fried chicken before, because she didn't clean off the feathers. He had suffered through some meals, but he was not eating that shit today.      He sat down on the couch and tried to relax, but he couldn't shake this eerie feeling that someone was watching him.

In fact, Chris had followed Brandon all day. He Knew that Brandon bought a gun from Tank. He had watched Brandon's every move, and he knew Brandon was scared. This was a battle that Brandon couldn't win. Chris ran the streets, and nothing got past him.

Chris dialed Brandon's cell phone. It was time for negotiations.

"Yeah," Brandon answered.

"Nigga, you ready to talk business?" Chris asked. " I want my half."

"I ain't giving you shit! Especially after you pulled that shit this morning! Fuck you!"

"I swear on your dead mother's grave, if you don't give me my half, you're going to be buried right next to her." And with that, Chris hung up the phone.

Chris handed the blunt back to Tank and got back in his car. Chris wanted Brandon to be strapped. If Brandon wanted to be a big man, it was time for time for him to see how big men played. He told Tank to sell Brandon the smallest gun he could. Deep down inside Chris didn't want to hurt Brandon. He just wanted to scare him.

"Who are you talking to like that?" Mia asked as she fixed him a plate. She brought it around to the couch and handed it to him.

He took one look at it and passed it back. "No , thank you, sweetie. I already ate."

Mia took the plate and threw it in the trash.

"You ate over her house, didn't you?" She began to cry. "I knew that's where you went."

"What the hell are you talking about?" Brandon's faced scrunched up. " I was out taking care of business. I wasn't with another woman."

She ran into the bedroom and shut the door.

Brandon waited a half hour before going after her. He figured she should have cooled off by then. He went into the bedroom and found her sitting on the side of the side whispering on the phone. She hung up as soon as she noticed Brandon standing there.

He took a seat and put his arm around her. Chris had got him good. Mia didn't trust him. His marriage was already on the rocks, and his beef with Chris was just making things worse.

"Baby, I wasn't with another woman. I promise you that," he said and kissed her on the cheek.

"My mother gave me the name of a marriage counselor. I think we should make an appointment," she said.

"Do you really think that we need a counselor?" he asked as he kissed her on the neck.

"After what happened this morning , we need a miracle."

Mia excused herself and went back into the kitchen.

She looked at the food she prepared. Who was she kidding? It looked awful, and she wouldn't have eaten it either. She threw it all away.

As Mia cleaned up the kitchen, Brandon took a shower and got into bed. He might as well just give Chris what he wanted. The only thing was that he only had about a million left, after paying all of his bills. Brandon was going to call Chris in the morning and put an end to this silly shit.

Mia came back into the room, dripping wet from taking her own shower. Times like these made Brandon feel like he had made the right choice by marrying Mia.

He pulled her wet, naked body on top of him. Kissing her, he then positioned her pussy on his face. He licked her pussy as she gyrated all over his face. He could tell that she was about to cum because her body stiffened. He quickly got up and began fucking her from behind. She came as soon as he stuck his dick inside her. He didn't care, as long as she was satisfied.

Brandon got up and lay beside her. Mia disappeared under the covers and began sucking his dick. It was so good that Brandon had to hold on to the bedpost. He ran his fingers through her hair as she bobbed up and down.

He began to moan when she started to lick his balls. "Oh, baby." He bit his Bottom lip. "Damn."

Mia came from under the covers and started to ride him Brandon bounced her up and down on his dick until he came. He cuddled Mia in his arms. He was just going to give Chris the money. He didn't want to fuck up what he already had at home.

Brandon slept until noon the next day. Mia was already up and dressed when he rolled over.

"Where are you going?" he asked.

Mia was applying her makeup. "We have a marriage coun-
seling session at two," she said.

Brandon grabbed his cell phone off the night table and
dialed Chris. "Meet me at the office in a half hour," Brandon
said. "Come alone, and no weapons." He hung up the phone.
Brandon dressed quickly and was almost out the door before
Mia caught him.

"Where are you going?" she asked.

"I'll be right back, he said.

"You know we have that meeting," she said.

"I'll be back way before then, he said and closed the door
behind him. He was just going to write a check to Chris for
the money he owed him.

Brandon drove to the old office and let himself in. Epic
had given him forty-five days to move out his shit. He had
taken all of his stuff before he left for the honeymoon, so
there was nothing there but a couple pictures and some office
furniture. He sat quietly and waited for Chris to show.


Mia watched from the parking lot as Brandon pulled off in
this gold Toyota Camry. Her suspicion was again getting the
better of her, so she hailed a cab and instructed the driver to
follow closely behind him. She overheard him saying he was
going to meet someone, and she was damned if another bitch
was going to have her man.

She instructed the driver to park right in front of the building. Mia paid the driver two hundred dollars to stay put. As
she waited, she saw Chris walking up and slouched down in
her seat.

Brandon heard the keys jingling in the lock. He checked
for his gun, and made sure it was tucked securely in his boot.

Chris came through the door nice and calm. He looked at
Brandon. "So where's my money?" he asked.

Brandon took the check out of the back pocket of this jeans and flicked it at him.

"Here," he said.

The check fell on the floor. Chris bent down to pick it up, and when he got back up Brandon was aiming the gun at him. Chris didn't think Brandon had the balls. He knew he should have carried his piece.

"Go ahead and shoot me, nigga, if you so tough," Chris said.

"I should fuckin' kill you," Brandon said. He looked at the gun and finally figured out how to cock it.

Chris took a step toward Brandon. He hated to be threatened. He rushed Brandon and tried to take the gun. They tussled back and forth until the gun finally discharged.

Brandon opened his mouth, but before he could say anything, he fell to the floor.

Chris looked down. Brandon was hit in the stomach.

"Oh, shit!" Chris said. "What did I do?"

Chris ran down the steps of the building and out onto the street. Mia was on the sidewalk in front of the building by now. He took one look at her and took off in the other direction.

Brandon stumbled down the steps behind Chris. Falling down the last flight. His clothes were stained with blood.

Mia started panting heavily. "Oh my God, somebody help me. Please!" She was screaming at the top of her lungs. "Call the police!"

Mia grabbed Brandon's heavy body and put his head in her lap. Blood was seeping out of his mouth as rocked him back and forth until the ambulance arrived,

Brandon's vision was blurry. He looked up at Mia. He could feel every one of her tears hitting his face.

The thought of Brandon not being by her side made her

crazy. "Baby, please don't die," shae said. " I love you. You can't leave me like this."


Chris ran for five blocks straight. His thoughts were so scrambled that when he looked up he was surprised to realize he was standing in front of the police station. The gray stone walls gave hime the chills. He pulled out a cigarette from his pocket and lit it. He took two long drags and exhaled.

*What the hell just happened?* Chris wondered. He rambled through his back pocket and pulled out the bloodstained check. He shook his head. "One million dollars," he said ou loud. He folded it back up and put it away. He took one last drag from the cigarette and put it out on the bottom of his shoe.

Chris walked into the police station and waited at the front desk.

"Can I help you?" the police officer asked.

"Y-y-yes," Chris stuttered. "I'm here to turn my self in."

# Prologue

Chris sat at the foot of Tank's bed and folded his hands. His eyesight was somewhat blurred, and his heart was beating so fast, he was starting to scare himself. The X pill he took had him buzzin' all crazy. He lay back on the bed and tried to allow his heart rate to slow down.

An annoying rumbling sound broke his concentration. He couldn't tell where it was coming from; it seemed muffled, so it was hard for him to track it down.

He jumped up from the bed and looked around the room. Finally, he realized it was coming from the TV stand. He reached over and grabbed the cell phone. He was going to throw it on the bed so he didn't have to hear the noise anymore, but he looked at the caller ID and saw Brandon's number.

He flipped the phone open. "Yo," he said, disguising his voice.

"That nigga dead yet?" Brandon asked, anxiously waiting for a response.

Chris closed the phone shut and placed it back on top of the television. His mind racing, he bent down and searched his bag for the Glock he'd stashed inside. He started to get nervous; it wasn't there.

"Looking for this?" Tank asked, holding the gun up for Chris to see. Smiling mischievously, Tank aimed at him and pretended to shoot.

Chris's eyes hardened in anger. He slid his hand in his boot and pulled out the switchblade he always kept for emergencies. His vision was still somewhat blurry, but it was coming back into focus real quick. He held it by his side and stood up.

Chris's first instinct was to charge him, but after what happened between him and Brandon, he decided that wouldn't be a good idea.

"I can't believe you going out like this," Chris said, walking slowly toward Tank.

"Nigga, please. Can you believe that I'm about to come up a cool mil by laying you down?" Tank asked, his finger resting on the trigger.

"So after all the shit I did for you and ya mom, you gonna take me out just like that, huh?" Chris inched closer in Tank's direction.

"After all you *did*? Nigga, is you crazy? You call fucking my moms and giving her a couple of dollars here and there doing something?" Tank waved the gun in his face. "What you thought, I didn't know you was fucking my moms? Nigga, I should plant one right in ya head for that shit right there alone."

Chris's mouth tightened as his eyes zeroed in on Tank's. He noticed Tank's hand was trembling.

Tank aimed the gun at Chris's head and slowly squeezed down on the trigger, but Chris dove for the floor, and the bullet grazed the side of his temple, leaving a small half-inch tear in his flesh.

Chris jumped back up so fast, it startled Tank, who dropped the gun to the floor. He flicked open his switchblade and stabbed Tank in the upper chest. "Nigga, I raised your ass," he said, twisting the knife inside Tank.

"Fuck you!" Tank took his last bit of energy and spat in Chris's face.

"No, fuck you!" Chris took the knife out of Tank's lifeless body, allowing him to fall to the floor.

Tank's mother rushed down the hall. "What's going on in there?" It wasn't the first time she heard Tank let a shot off in the house, but it was the first time she had ever heard him and Chris argue.

"Nothing," Chris replied. "Go sit down somewhere."

Following his orders, she shuffled back down the hallway to the living room and laid back down on the couch.

Chris grabbed a T-shirt from the bedroom floor and wiped the blood from his face. He then wrapped the T-shirt around his head and tied a knot in the back, He grabbed the Glock Tank had taken from him and stuffed it back in his bag. Then he grabbed the pound of weed and the two kilos of coke from the TV stand and placed them in his bag alongside the handgun.

After searching every inch of Tank's room, Chris came across an envelope of money taped to the bottom of the dresser drawer. He placed the envelope in his bag with the rest of his belongings Chris started toward the bedroom door. He closed it behind himself and walked casually down the hall to the living room past Brenda, and out the front door.

When Brenda rushed back down the hallway and swung the door to Tank's room open wide, she noticed her son laid out on the side of the bed, his eyes rolled in the back of his head. She started to scream.

She ran after Chris who was now outside the apartment and in the main hallway. "You son of a bitch! What did you do to my son?"

"Didn't I tell your ass to go sit down somewhere?" Chris grabbed Brenda by the arm and pushed her back into the apartment.

He closed back the door to the apartment and headed for

the stairwell. He took the bag down to the ground floor and out the side door. He placed his hood on his head and the bag on his back.

Chris strolled down the street without a care in the world, his hands in his pocket. He wasn't mad at Tank for trying to off him. In fact, he was impressed that he had enough heart to set him up. As for Brandon, it was already obvious as to what needed to be done. He'd broken every code that Chris lived by. Never in a million years did he think Brandon would put a price out on his head. It was time for Chris to show him who he was really fucking with.

"Every idle word that men shall speak,
they shall give account thereof in the day of judgment."
-Matthew 12:36

# Chapter 1

## The Quiet after the Storm
### May 2006

### Brandon

Brandon's eyes slowly fluttered open and closed as he tried to adjust himself to the glaring florescent lights shining in his face. Realizing he wasn't in the comfort of his own home, his eyes frantically scanned the room. *What am I doing lying in a hospital bed? And why is Mia boo-hooing so hard?*

He looked over to his right and saw Ms. Ruth sitting with her Bible in hand; she too was full of tears. Brandon wanted to get up and find out what was going on. He pushed with all his might to sit up, but he just couldn't. A sharp, intense pain shot through his right side, forcing him to lay still. He tried to say something, but nothing came out. He opened his eyes wide, trying to gain the attention of either one of the two, to alert them of his consciousness.

Finally, Ms. Ruth looked up and noticed Brandon's stare. She dropped her Bible to the floor in excitement and grabbed his hand tight. She sighed in relief. "Praise the Lord."

The thought of Brandon dying at the hand of her only son Chris was a burden she just couldn't stand to bear. Plus, Brandon was like a son to her; she had practically raised him after his mother died. She'd promised Brandon's mother that she would always care for him, and she wasn't about to let her down now.

She smiled as his warm eyes met hers. It was a feeling only a mother could experience, a feeling of joy and pain, the joy of seeing him alive, the pain of having to deal with what was still to come.

Just an hour ago, Ms. Ruth had gotten word that Chris was spotted in their old neighborhood. He was now a fugitive of the law, a wanted man. Part of her wanted to kill Chris herself. She would rather him die by her hand than that of the law. But she was a God-fearing woman who knew that his Day of Judgment would be by the hand of the Lord and His alone.

Noticing Ms. Ruth's enthusiasm, Mia rushed over to Brandon. Gently pushing Ms. Ruth aside, she threw herself across his limp body, her pregnant belly rubbing up against Brandon's chest. Mia then grabbed his partially bearded face and kissed him lovingly on the lips. She found herself becoming lost in his deep brown eyes; she missed him so much, she almost forgot how beautiful they were.

It was all coming back to Brandon now: the tussle with Chris at the office and the deafening sound of the gun as it struck him in the stomach. A sharp pain gushed through his right side as he relived the painful moments leading up to being shot by his best friend. Yes, it was he who pulled the gun and threatened to take Chris's life, but Chris was the one who should have caught a bullet. Chris had raped Brandon's wife and betrayed their friendship; he deserved to die.

Instead, he was the one who caught the bullet, and if it wasn't for Mia following him, his life would be over. She was definitely a rider and had proved in so many ways that she loved her man. Mia could have walked away when she'd found out about Lynn and the other baby, but she chose to stick around and make it work.

Brandon wanted to tell Mia he loved her, but every time he tried to open his mouth, nothing came out but a few short grunts. He pulled the IV out of his arm in frustration, but the nurse was quickly at his side to reinsert it.

"Glad to see you're awake." The nurse smiled, walking into the hospital room, overcrowded with all sorts of floral arrangements and fruit baskets.

There was barely enough room for Brandon, let alone Mia and Ms. Ruth. Not a day went by that Brandon didn't receive a get-well gesture from somebody. He was a well-liked man among the ladies.

The nurse continued over to the bed and took his temperature, which was regular. She then pulled out her stethoscope and proceeded to check his heartbeat and respiratory rates, which were also normal.

"Mr. Brunson, if you can hear me, blink your eyes two times," the nurse said, carefully placing the tube back into his arm.

Brandon blinked his eyes twice in confirmation. His grunts became louder as she pressed the tube firmly back into his flesh. He tried to push her away, but his body gave way in weakness. *This has to be a dream, a nightmare*, he thought. There was no way he was laying in a hospital on his deathbed. As a matter of fact he hated hospitals; one had killed his mother.

"The doctor will be in shortly," the nurse said, making sure the IV was securely in place. She turned to Mia. "Please keep an eye on him. That morphine drip is what's easing his pain." She placed the covers back over Brandon and left the room.

Sitting back down in the seat next to the bed, Ms. Ruth picked her Bible up off the floor, opened it to where she left off, and resumed reading the scriptures. Her prayers had been answered, and even though Brandon was still in bad shape, she had faith that he would make a full recovery.

Mia slowly paced back and forth, nervous about the doctor coming to check on Brandon. The last time he did a full checkup, he'd stated that there was a possibility that Brandon would not recover from his coma. Major complications arose after the surgery to remove the bullet from his abdomen. Brandon was fine at first, but a blood vessel ruptured, causing major hemorrhaging.

Mia's pacing came to an end as Dr. White entered the room. She took a seat on the bed next to Brandon and braced herself for the news.

Brandon ogled the chiseled-face fair-skinned man as he made his way over to his bedside. He could feel the tension in the room; both Mia and Ms. Ruth wore looks of extreme concern.

Dr. White peered over Brandon's body in his stainless steel half-rimmed frames and pulled out a pocket light. He flashed it into Brandon's eyes. He then checked Brandon's reflexes. There was no response when he hit both of Brandon's knees with the reflex hammer. He wrote something on his clipboard and continued with the evaluation. He asked Brandon to open his mouth wide and flashed the light inside. He then went back to writing on the clipboard.

After what seemed like hours to Mia and Ms. Ruth, Dr. White was finally finished. He stood by and continued writing on his clipboard as he always did before he addressed the family with the prognosis. He pulled his glasses from his face and placed them in his jacket pocket; he then placed the clipboard under his arm.

Mia's heart thudded as Dr. White parted his lips to speak. She was now clasping Brandon's arm with all her strength.

"Ms. Brunson, we're going to run a few tests and take some blood samples," Dr. White started. "He may have to learn how to walk and talk again, but he should be fine." He cracked a half-smile as he proceeded to the door. "The nurses will be in shortly to draw those samples," he said before walking out.

"Thank you, Doctor," Mia exclaimed.

Mia and Ms. Ruth had been by Brandon's side faithfully for the last two months. Mia was eight months pregnant and due to have the baby within the next month. Instead of staying on bed rest like her doctor prescribed, she was up every day at the crack of dawn, preparing to spend the day with her husband at the hospital.

She rubbed her hand through Brandon's untamed mane; his curly hair wisped through her fingers with ease. Mia was so delighted at the thought of having her husband back; she missed him greatly.

Mia had indeed chosen Brandon as her man, but he often carried the thought that he had chosen her, and she often spent most of her days daydreaming about the life they used to live.

Mia had seen Brandon at a professional networking event for young blacks and fell in love with him. She had just signed a million-dollar contract with Elite Modeling Agency and was on her way out of the country for her first photo shoot. He didn't really know who she was at that point and had seen her a couple of times around town, but that was it.

Even though she was out of the country for months at a time, it didn't stop her from hiring a private investigator to find out about her mystery man. She wanted to know everything about Brandon, from what kind of friends he kept to his favorite cocktail, and had him followed for several months before she decided to approach him.

When Chris approached her about meeting up with Brandon for the first time, she knew at that moment that she was destined to be with him. She'd already had plans on introducing herself to him, but this made it easier.

Chris had told her that Brandon had inquired about her but hadn't had the time to make things happen due to him working nonstop on getting the record label off the ground. He'd told her he could provide the right opportunity to make the hookup, if she did a little something for him. All she had to do was give him some pussy, and he would introduce her, with no problem.

Mia would have usually said no to an offer like that, but she knew they were close and that Brandon would trust Chris's judgment of her. So she hooked up with Chris and gave him the best ride of his life. Chris was so turned out, he was trying to persuade her to date him instead of Brandon, but Mia insisted that he keep his part of the bargain.

Plus, Chris was too hood for her; he had no class. She wanted a man who knew about fine wines and expensive art.

The night she officially met Brandon for the first time was magical. They instantly had a vibe that Mia knew would be unbreakable. Yes, she fucked him on the first date; she just couldn't resist.

Mia remembered it like it was yesterday. Brandon's smooth chocolate skin and full, succulent lips lured her in. And his big dick sealed the deal. Although it had been just over a year since they met, she never forgot how good he felt inside of her for the first time. When he'd slid his dark, hardened member inside her, she swore for God she saw heaven. There was no way she was going to allow him to get away from her.

Mia was actually engaged to be married to someone else when she'd met Brandon. But she called it off the next morning, after her first date with Brandon in Atlantic City. She briefly told Brandon about her previous plans to marry, but if he knew that she was engaged when they met, she would have never become Mrs. Brandon Brunson. Mia was thankful for the life she lived. She'd snagged herself a man who knew how to negotiate in the boardroom and fuck the hell out of her in the bedroom.


Mia slid off the bed and made sure not to wake Brandon. She was fighting the urge to wake him up; she wanted to spend every second of the day with him now that he was out of his coma. He had missed so much over the last few months—how much her belly had grown, and the first few times the baby kicked in her stomach. His daughter was ready to come busting out of the womb any day now.

She dug around in her Gucci tote bag for the ultrasound pictures and placed them on his bedside table. She then went into the bathroom and closed the door behind her.

Brandon's eyes opened at the sound of the screeching bathroom door. He noticed Mia was no longer at his side and began to grunt loudly.

"It's okay," Ms. Ruth consoled him. "Everything is going to be okay," she said, patting his arm. She continued to read her Bible.

Brandon wanted to believe what Ms. Ruth was saying, but he knew otherwise. He knew that a long road to recovery was ahead and that his life would no longer be the same. The only brother he knew was no longer considered family.

Six months ago, while Brandon was away making business deals in New York to further their careers, Chris was back home having his way with Brandon's wife. Brandon trusted Chris to hold things down while he was away and never thought he was capable of something like this. He always knew Chris was a fucked-up dude, but he took it too far, robbing him of his happily-ever-after. He would no longer be the man of substance he was known as, but a coward who allowed some street thug to violate his wife and take his manhood, all in a matter of months.

Brandon vowed at that moment that, if he ever recovered from this ordeal, he wouldn't make the same mistake as before. He loved Ms. Ruth like his own mother, but that bastard son of hers was in the way of progress and was better off dead than alive.

Brandon sat up in his hospital bed and watched the early morning news. It had been three weeks since he awoke from his coma, and he was coming along very well because of his great physical shape. His speech had already returned in full swing, and he'd been working hard with the physical therapist to fine-tune his mobile skills. Brandon was able to walk with the help of a cane, which was more than enough for him. And with every passing day, he felt more confident about his recovery.

Brandon listened closely as the news began to report a robbery at the Crazy Market, a local store across the street from the projects where he grew up. He grabbed the remote control and turned the volume up as high as it would go. He'd missed most of the report, fumbling with the remote, but he did recognize the face in the surveillance video. He could tell by the long, red braids that extended to the middle of his back.

Brandon sucked his teeth. Chris's stupidity never seemed to amaze him. Chris was the only nigga in the hood with reddish-brown hair, and Brandon had begged him to cut that shit time and time again, telling him that hair was going to get him in trouble.

He smirked as he reached over to the table beside him, picked up the phone, and started dialing.

"Hello. Nine-one-one," an operator answered after the second ring.

"Yes, I want to call in a tip," Brandon said, a wicked smile spreading across his face.

"Go ahead," the operator said, "I'm listening."

"The guy who robbed the Crazy Market name is Chris Black," he blurted out, giving his whole government name to the law. "He's known around the way as Chief."

Brandon quickly placed the receiver back on the cradle, making sure not to give the operator the time to ask him any more questions. He moved his bed to its original position and gloated, amused with himself.

*Chris must be real desperate, sticking up corner stores,* Brandon thought.

Chris had money; a million dollars, to be exact. The problem was, if he tried to cash the check, the cops would scoop his ass up. Brandon had been checking his account on a daily basis just to make sure it was still there. He knew Chris would rather chalk that mill up as a loss and make his money back on the street than to risk getting locked up.

Brandon was already one step ahead of him. He'd called ahead to Tank and offered him a cool million to take Chris out. If things went the way they were supposed to, he'd be gone by the end of next week. Chris was living on borrowed time, and Brandon was loving every minute of it.

He looked over at the clock on his bedside table; it was almost time for his workout with the physical therapist. He closed his eyes and tried to relax.

Just as he was nodding off, Amy, his physical therapist, appeared in the doorway. She knocked lightly before entering the room.

Brandon opened his eyes and waved for her to come in. She closed the door behind her, locked it, and leaned against it in a seductive manner. She smiled deviously as she pulled her lab coat open and revealed her tanned, naked body, her plump breasts standing at attention, her phat pussy neatly trimmed, like a landing strip. Brandon's wood hardened at the thought of landing his plane right in between her thighs.

"Are you ready for your workout?" she said, dropping her coat to the floor.

Brandon looked at her well-sculpted body and licked his lips; he was definitely ready to get worked over. He enjoyed his sessions with Amy. They'd been going at it strong for the past two weeks. He'd even requested a room at the end of the corridor for extra privacy, explaining to the staff that the room he previously stayed in was too noisy and gave him headaches.

He knew it was only a matter of time before he got that ass. Amy had been flirting with him since he'd started his rehabilitation plan. She would bend over from time to time during the sessions, and to his delight, she wouldn't have any panties on. Brandon would look up, and her phat white pussy would be planted dead in his face.

One day they were doing exercises on the floor with the cardio ball, and Brandon decided to try his luck. He was sitting on the floor, and she was sitting in front of him on the ball with her legs wide open. Brandon lifted her jacket up just enough to slide his tongue between the lips of her pussy. She moaned and groaned as Brandon wiggled his tongue around in a circular motion. He didn't demand anything from her that day; he just wanted to make sure she was game to try it again

.The next day Amy showed at his room, on her day off, in a pair of black crotchless panties and fire engine-red stilettos. They went at it so hard, Brandon had a red lipstick stain around his dick for three days. He made sure to stay in bed around Mia so she wouldn't see it.

"Bring that ass over here to daddy." Brandon patted the small space between him and the edge of the bed.

Amy sauntered over to the hospital bed, climbed on top of him, and planted a long, inviting kiss on his lips. Weaving her tongue in and out of his mouth, she began biting his bottom lip. Amy rubbed his tightly sculpted chest, her pussy moistening.

Brandon had something else in mind for her to bite on, and it sure wasn't his lips. Pushing her head down toward his throbbing hard on, he watched as she accepted him into her mouth. She licked up and down his erect penis as if it was a Popsicle, massaging his balls at the same time.

Brandon watched as she spat on his erection and sucked him off like a vacuum cleaner. His eyes rolled in the back of his head as she slobbered on his manhood. He just couldn't help himself. Amy had the best head game Brandon had ever experienced.

Releasing himself on her lips, he watched as she slurped it off. "Did you bring one?" he asked.

"I got it right here, baby." Amy got up and grabbed her lab coat from the floor. She searched around in the coat pocket and returned to his side with the condom in her hand.

Brandon cracked a sly grin as Amy opened the package and placed the condom on her lips. He watched in amazement as she carefully applied the condom to his swollen member with her mouth.

Positioning herself over him, she pushed his hard-on deep inside her drenched walls. She moaned heavily as he filled her to capacity.

Brandon grabbed her tiny size four waist and guided her in several hurried thrusts, causing her to whine. He then positioned the hospital bed upright and continued pounding her petite frame against his.

Amy grabbed the hospital guardrail in hopes of slowing him down, but he smacked her hand away from the rail. He then grabbed her long bleach-blonde hair and began pulling it. "Tell Daddy how good this dick is," he said, putting a firmer grasp on her hair.

"Oooh, Daddy, your dick is so good!" Amy tried to kiss him on the lips, but he moved his face, allowing it to land on his cheek.

He liked Amy and all, but he wasn't into kissing her. He'd allowed her to kiss him today and a couple of times before, but he was really trying to break her out of it. She was a "smut jawn," and he knew she probably fucked other dudes. Besides, kissing was for people in love, and Brandon was far from in love with her.

Amy had been begging him to eat her out again, but he refused each time. Yes, he did it once before, but that was just to get the ass. He regretted it then because there was a not-so-nice odor he encountered while doing it. Brandon chalked it up and took one for the team. He figured she was probably sweaty down there from being at work all day.

Continuing to guide Amy as she rode his dick, Brandon suddenly became bored. She just wasn't throwing it the way he wanted it. He wanted the "animal fuck" she gave him when they'd first started messing around. Now, she was stroking him like she was starting to catch feelings.

He knew this was going to have to be the last time they fucked. If he wanted to make love, he would be fucking his wife instead. He took his hands off of Amy's waist and placed them behind his head in a restless manner. Already knowing he wasn't going to cum, his fascination with her was over. He closed his eyes and allowed her to continue to get her shit off.

Amy slowed up, noticing his lack of interest. Brandon's usually bright eyes were now gloomy and hollow. "What's wrong?"

"Nothing," Brandon responded dryly. He grabbed her hips again, bringing her back up to speed.

Brandon knew that Amy was just a snack to feed his appetite for women. Her time was up, and from the frown on her face, she knew it.

He'd come to a conclusion about his relationship with Mia also. It wasn't that he didn't love her; it was just that he was a man who liked to be loved by a lot of women. And being with only one was just not enough for him. He would always be a ladies' man—he loved pussy and it was that simple.

And he had no problem getting it. Brandon always seemed to be able to get away with murder because of his looks. His muscular frame and dark chocolate complexion made even the most committed woman rethink her relationship. He was as equally charming; he made sure that when he was with a woman he made her feel like she was the only one alive. And owning his own record label and being an Ivy League graduate were added perks to his package. So Mia had to either get in line or roll out, but he knew was too loyal and would never leave him.

Mia walked slowly down to Brandon's room, which was stationed at the end of the hallway. She had great news to share. The doctors had finally agreed to induce her labor, and she was scheduled to have the baby tomorrow morning. Mia was thrilled because Brandon would be able to witness the birth of his first child and she would have him there to support her.

She stopped midway down the hall to catch her breath when she heard strange panting noises coming from the direction in which she was headed. As she continued down the empty corridor, the sounds became clearer.

Mia tried to focus on her footsteps, making sure not to

make more noise than she had to. At eight and a half months pregnant, she was still strutting in her heels.

"Fuck me, baby!" Amy screamed, pinching her swollen nipples.

Brandon decided to give it back to her so she could cum faster and get the hell out of his room. He hammered her small frame against his body, pushing himself deeper into her sweetness. He placed his middle finger at the tip of her asshole and massaged it carefully until his entire finger was submerged in her ass.

Mia placed her ear against the door. The moans were even louder than before. She cracked the door just enough to peep inside the room, and she couldn't believe her eyes. She had to blink twice. Brandon's physical therapist was bouncing up and down on her man like a jackrabbit in heat.

Mia quietly closed the door and slid down to the floor. Tears flowed freely down her face. After all she had done for him, he still had to go and fuck another woman. Mia's eyes glazed over, and her salty tears of sorrow turned into tears of rage. She was going to fix that nigga. If she couldn't have him, then no one else would either.

Mia carefully got up from the floor, brushed her clothes off, and made her way back in the opposite direction. Brandon was a dog, and in her mind every dog has his day. She was going to make sure he got his; she just didn't know how. She decided she would play things differently this time. She was going to act as if nothing happened. It would be better this way. Plus, when she did get him, he wouldn't suspect it coming.

# Chapter 2

## Hiding Out

### Chris

Beads of sweat dripped from Chris's brow as he forced open the back window to his mother's house. He made sure not to make too much noise; it was early afternoon, and the residents in his mother's neighborhood in the far northeast had no problem with calling the cops. She was one of only two black persons on the block, with the exception of the interracial couple that lived directly across from her.

Chris hoisted himself up and through the window, and fell on the kitchen floor. He gathered himself, dusted off, and headed upstairs to his old room. He needed clean clothes and a shower. It had been days since he'd eaten or had anywhere safe to lay his head.

The cops had found out about his room at the Blue Moon Motel and had been staking it out ever since. He was pretty sure they would be watching his mother's house next. He planned on staying for no more than a few hours because he knew anything longer would just be too risky. He opened the door to his old room, and it was just the way he left it. His clothes were still neatly placed in the closet and his shoes aligned at the foot of the bed. He pulled an old Rocawear sweat suit from the closet and laid it on the bed. He then went over to the dresser and pulled open the top drawer. From the five pairs of boxers neatly arranged in a row, he pulled a pair out of the drawer and placed it on the bed also.

Chris then proceeded down the hall to the bathroom to take a shower. He pulled off his dingy, gray T-shirt and placed it on the toilet seat as he waited for the shower water to run warm. He dropped his jeans to his ankles but realized he was yet to take off his boots.

As Chris bent down and unlaced his shoes, he realized the soles of his muddy boots had stained his mother's light blue bath mat. He could smell the strong musky odor that filled the bathroom as he stripped down to his boxers. He reached his hand in the shower and tested the water. When it was nice and hot, he jumped in the shower and allowed the water to moisten his body. He grabbed the soap and lathered it up on the washrag. He then proceeded to scrub himself clean. Chris felt relieved; it was if all of his sins were being washed from his body.

For the first time in his life, though, his conscience was doing a job on him. Chris wished with all his heart that he could turn back the hands of time. He would have never charged Brandon that day at the office. He knew Brandon didn't have the heart to use the gun, but when he pulled it out, something just made him go crazy.

Chris pounded his fist against the damp shower tiles. He knew he should've paid more attention to the signs.

The first argument they had over money was definitely an indication that something was wrong. Confronting Brandon about the missing money had led to a scuffle. Chris's temper got the better of him then, and he wound up giving Brandon a busted lip. He and Brandon stopped talking for a while over that incident, and Chris found his comfort in alcohol. Scotch, to be exact.

Every time he thought about what he had done to Brandon, it caused him to drink, and this time was no different. He was ashamed of the person he'd become. There was a time when he would do anything for Brandon, watching his back in the streets and making sure he never wanted a thing. In fact, he always felt that Brandon had the better chance of getting out of the projects and hoped that when he did, he would never forget who helped him.

When they'd started the record label, Chris saw a new way of life. A legal hustle. He was able to make just as much money with the label as he did in the streets, but there was one problem. The allure of the game kept calling. Chris loved hustling; it was really the only thing he was truly good at. Selling weight came natural to him, and when it was time to go to war, he didn't have a problem squeezing a trigger.

Chris finished up his shower and dried off. He wrapped the towel around his waist and gathered his clothing from the bathroom floor. He figured he could probably sneak a quick nap before his mom got home.

Chris opened the door to the bathroom and was met by a thick smog of pepper spray.

"Arrrggghhh!" he yelled, dropping his clothes on the floor and running back into the bathroom.

He doused his face with water in hopes of stopping the stinging sensation that was causing him to not be able to open his eyes.

When the burning finally left him, he opened his eyes and came face to face with his mother. Chris lowered his head in shame; he knew that she was disappointed in him. He wanted to change and often wished he could be a better person, but every time he tried to do right, something seemed to go wrong. He stood in silence and waited for her to make the first move.

Ms. Ruth stood in shock as she stared at her son for the first time in several months. Positioned stiffly against the upstairs railing, her emotions were sending her mixed signals. She didn't know if she wanted to hug Chris or smack him.

She continued down the hallway to her bedroom and shut the door behind her. Chris had caused so much pain in her life. Yes, she enjoyed her beautiful four-bedroom, two-car garage home in the far northeast her son had provided for her, but the way he'd done it made her uneasy.

She knew Chris sold drugs; in fact, she'd known for years. Ever since he was thirteen. They were living in the projects when she went in his room to make his bed one day after he'd left for school, and when she went to tuck the sheets under the mattress, she came across a wad of twenties in a rubber band and a small handgun. She ran out of that room as fast as her two feet could take her and never went back in again. Ms. Ruth never mentioned what she found to Chris. But that was just the beginning.

At the age of fifteen, he had dropped out of school and was staying out for days at a time. He was dealing full-time and had become the man of the house. Ms. Ruth hated that he was a hustler, but loved the money he was bringing home, so she ignored everything he did. When the cops came looking for him, she'd lie to cover for his whereabouts. She knew she would have to answer to God when her time came, but she had to protect her boy.

Chris hurried to his room, his thoughts of a catnap now out the window. He wanted to get out of his mother's house as quickly as possible. They hadn't exchanged words since she found him on his knees giving Kane, another man, head. She'd told Chris to leave that night, and he hadn't been back since. He so desperately wanted his relationship back with his mom; she was the only person in his life that kept him sane.

Chris quickly got dressed. He was supposed to meet up with Tank later on tonight. He grabbed his old bookbag from under the bed and placed the remaining outfits from the closet inside. When he turned to go out the door, his mother was standing in the walkway.

"I thought you turned yourself in," she said, looking him over thoroughly. His face was thinner than usual. The first thought that ran through her mind was that he was hooked on drugs.

"I tried to, Ma. I thought I was doing the right thing, but the more I thought about it, I realized that jail just ain't for me," Chris said, throwing the backpack over his shoulder. "I couldn't have nobody telling me when to eat, sleep, and shit."

"So where you been staying?" she asked, searching his eyes for an answer.

"Here and there," Chris responded, still trying to feel her out. He didn't know if she was asking because she cared, or because she was going to turn him in.

"I'm not going to turn you in," she said, sensing his uncertainty. "Why don't we go down to the kitchen, and I'll make you something to eat."

Chris tossed the knapsack on the bed and eased by her. He quickly made his way down to the kitchen. His stomach was doing backflips just thinking about his mother's cooking. She closed the door to his bedroom and followed him downstairs.

Chris sat at the kitchen table with his hands folded, patiently waiting to see what his mother was going to cook up. He watched carefully as she made her way around the kitchen.

She turned on the stove and placed a big black skillet on the burner, placed the grease in the pan, and allowed it to heat. She then walked over to the refrigerator and pulled out two big pieces of catfish. She seasoned them up and laid them neatly in the skillet.

Ms. Ruth then took a seat across from Chris at the table. There was so much she wanted to ask him, and so little time to do so. She knew he couldn't stay long; she just wanted to make sure that he left with a good meal in his stomach and some pocket money, though she didn't have much to give.

She excused herself from the table and went to grab her purse from the living room sofa. Ms. Ruth counted the money in her wallet; there was only sixty dollars in it. She closed it back up and placed it on the coffee table. She then remembered the money she'd stashed in her nightstand drawer. She didn't know how much was there, but she did know that it would be enough for him to find a place to stay. She went up to her room and pulled out the stack of cash which was made up of mostly twenties and hundreds in a rubber band.

Ms. Ruth went back down stairs to the kitchen and plopped the money on the table in front of Chris. She sat back down across from him.

"What is that?" he said, looking at the money.

"Take it. It's all I have."

"I don't want your money." He shook his head and pushed the money back toward her.

"Son, this is your money," she said, pushing it back in front of him.

"Remember all that money you used to give me to pay bills?" she asked, getting up to check on the catfish.

"Yeah, I remember," he said, still somewhat confused.

"Well, that's it. I saved it." She glanced over at him as she continued cooking.

"Ma, I-I-I can't," he stammered, looking at the large wad of cash.

"Yes, you can. Please take it." She walked back over to the
table and sat down. She took his hand in hers. "Take the
money, Chris. I want you to have it." She placed it in his hand
and pushed it toward him. She then got up from the table
and went back over to the stove.

Chris unwrapped the cash and counted it. His eyes wid-
ened as he passed the five thousand mark. *Mom must have been
stacking for a long time.* When he finished counting, the money
totaled twelve grand. And with the money he'd gotten his
hands on from sticking up the Crazy Market, he had enough
to cop a few bricks and amp up his cash flow. It was time to
put the team back on the street and move some product. If
he had to lie low and do some dirt to get back on top, then so
be it. This was going to change his life and make everything
better. He could move around better with the right amount
of cash, and if he was to get caught for shooting Brandon or
selling coke, he could afford to pay a good-ass lawyer to get
him off.

Chris stuffed the money in the pocket on his sweatpants.
He couldn't believe his mother had held on to all of that
money. He was sure she was using it to pay her bills.

He watched as his mom heated up some leftovers to go
with his catfish. When she was done, there was a big plate
filled with catfish, rice and beans, macaroni and cheese, and
corn bread sitting in front of him. He dug right in without
saying a word.

Ms. Ruth watched as he devoured his plate in big bites.
Cooking for Chris was her way of telling him that she still
loved him.

As soon as Chris took the first bite, he knew he had his
mother back by his side. He knew that he would never be perfect; no one was. But he did know, just by the simple meal she
prepared, that she loved him with all of her heart and would
always be there for him.

The telephone on the wall by the kitchen rang, and Chris picked it up. What could he be thinking? He was on the run.

"Hello," he said, his mouth full of catfish.

"Hello. Who the hell is this?"

"You called here. Who the fuck is you?" Chris continued chewing his macaroni and cheese.

Mia sucked her teeth. "Is Ms. Ruth there?" *Who the hell would be answering her phone?* Then it quickly dawned on her. She hung up the phone and dialed the police as fast as she could.

Chris hung up the phone and shrugged it off as a prank call.

"Who was that?" Ms. Ruth asked, cleaning the kitchen.

Chris licked his fingers. "Wrong number, I guess." He got up from the table and placed his dish in the sink. He then went over to the refrigerator and grabbed a can of Pepsi. After popping the top, he took a swig from the can and sat back down at the table.

Chris was really considering taking that nap again. He looked at the clock on the microwave; it was early evening, and he had a couple of hours to kill. He left the kitchen table and went to stretch out on the couch. He flicked on the TV. *The Simpsons* was just coming on. Propping his feet up on the coffee table, he allowed the couch to swallow him up, and after just a few short minutes, he was snoring.

Ms. Ruth watched as he slept peacefully. Seeing Chris tonight had lifted a burden off of her shoulders. She'd rather accept him as he was than not have him in her life altogether. She sat down beside him and rested her weary body.

Ms. Ruth was so busy tending to Brandon and Chris, she'd never told them that she was sick. Under the circumstances, she'd rather keep it to herself than trouble them with the news of her heart condition. She closed her eyes and sat silently. For the first time in several months she was at peace.

***

The police officer pounded on the front door, causing the front windows to shake. "Open up!"

Ms. Ruth opened her eyes and leaped to her feet, her heart pounding. She patted Chris on the arm, and before he could say a word, she covered his mouth with her hand. "The cops are out there. You gotta get out of here," she whispered, signaling for Chris to go upstairs.

Chris jumped to his feet and tiptoed up the steps to his room. He grabbed the backpack off the bed and threw it on his shoulder. He opened the bedroom window and stepped out on the ledge. His room was located directly over the shed. Chris looked down at the ground; he could make the jump easily. All he had to do was make sure he planted his feet right when he hit the ground. He braced himself for the landing and jumped over the side of the ledge. To his surprise, the cops didn't have anyone covering the back of the house. He then took off down the alleyway as fast as his feet could take him.

Ms. Ruth peeked out the front blinds and saw two big burly black plainclothes cops and one scrawny white uniformed officer waiting for her to answer the door. One of the cops seemed very familiar to her. She remembered him from the last time Chris was in trouble with the law. She took one last look up the steps and prayed to God that Chris had made it out okay.

After several more hard knocks, she finally answered the door slowly. "Can I help you?"

"Ma'am, we have a warrant for a Mr. Christopher Black." The uniformed officer flashed a white envelope in her face as they all pushed past her and into the house.

She stood by the door and watched as they searched the downstairs portion of the house. They threw the pillows off her couch and onto the floor. The uniformed officer was searching in her kitchen cabinets, opening each spice tin one at a time and leaving them uncovered on the counter.

The plainclothes cops started for the stairs.

"Wait, you can't go up there." Ms. Ruth blocked the steps with her frail, aging body.

"Ma'am, please move out of the way." The white uniformed officer joined them in the living room.

Ms. Ruth moved to the side and stood at the bottom of the steps and waited for them to open Chris's door. Her heart thumped as they busted in the bedroom with their guns drawn.

"Nothing in here," the uniformed officer said, his eyes darting around the room.

Noticing the opened window, he rushed over and stuck his head out to see if there were any signs that Chris had used it as an exit. There was nothing within eyes' view but a scrounged dog sifting through a torn bag of trash. The officer then made his way down the hall to Ms. Ruth's room.

Ms. Ruth let out a sigh of relief. She thought she was getting too old for this nonsense. The law knocking at her door was nothing new to her; it was just that, in her current condition, the excitement was taking a toll on her body. She was beginning to sweat, and her heart was practically beating out of her chest. The room was now spinning.

She forgot all about the cops searching her house and lay down on the couch. Ms. Ruth closed her eyes and prayed for God to allow her to at least make it until she could get the boys back together. They needed each other, especially if she wasn't going to be around too much longer to care for them.

*\*\*\**

Chris panted as he stopped to catch his breath. After running seven blocks straight on a full stomach, he dropped his backpack to the ground and leaned against the bricked alley wall. He surveyed his surroundings. There was a 7-Eleven at the left opening of the alley and an apartment complex at the other. He was sure to find a phone booth at the 7-Eleven, and he could call Tank to pick him up.

Chris walked slowly up the alleyway, making sure to look over his shoulder here and there. The stench of piss and alcohol burned his nose as he crept up toward the left end of the alley. When he reached the end of the opening, he noticed a police car sitting in the parking lot. There wasn't an officer inside, but he knew that one was most likely somewhere close by.

He walked over to the phone booth and picked up the receiver. He then dug into his pocket for some change. Hovering over the phone booth, he put two quarters in, and dialed Tank's cell phone.

"Yo," Tank answered on the first ring.

"Yo, nigga," he said, looking over his shoulder, "it's Chief. I need you to come scoop me."

"Where you at?"

Chris was still scoping out his surroundings. "I'm at the 7-Eleven on Rising Sun Avenue."

"I'll be there in twenty minutes." Tank loaded his pistol and tucked it his pants. He pulled his shirt back over his jeans to show no signs that he was packing.

Chris watched the officer walk out of the convenience store with a jelly donut in his hand. He nodded to acknowledge Chris and got in his squad car.

Chris nodded back and turned toward the alleyway, the receiver still in his hand. Even though Tank had already hung up, he still waited for the cop to pull off. "A'ight. Cool, man." Chris finally rested the receiver on the hook just as the officer backed out of the parking lot.

Posting up on the side of the building, Chris could feel the sweat pouring from his forehead. He wiped his face with his hand and placed his hands in his pocket, his eyes scanning the parking lot.

Several people had walked past him, and he felt as if they were staring. He pulled his hood over his head to conceal his face, hoping no one recognized him from the surveillance video of the market robbery.

Chris was drunk and high off X when he'd robbed that market. He just walked in the store without any type of mask to hide his face and stuck it up. The cashier at the counter was scared to death when Chris waved the gun in his face. And when he heard him cock it, the cashier opened the drawer and cleaned it out. Chris came out with the cash and didn't even bother to run. He walked off and didn't look back.

Tank pulled up in the parking lot of the 7-Eleven in his '98 Caprice and honked the horn.

Chris looked over at the car and was impressed by how his young bull was riding. He walked around the side of Tank's tinted out whip sitting on 22's, gliding his hand across the custom candy apple red paint job. He grinned. He'd taught Tank all too well. Tank took everything Chris taught him and made it work for him. He continued around to the passenger side of the car and got in.

Tank shifted the car into drive, turned the volume of the music up to the max, and sped off, leaving skid marks in the parking lot. He took Rising Sun Avenue down to Roosevelt Boulevard and jumped on the expressway, heading back to North Philly.

Chris was finally able to relax. He threw his bag in the back seat and took the hood off his head.

Tank sifted around in his pocket and pulled out a Dutch and a dime bag of weed. He tossed it onto Chris's lap and refocused his attention on the expressway.

Chris grabbed both the Dutch and the weed from his lap and instantly went to work. He opened the Dutch and split it carefully down the center. He then emptied the filling onto the floor of Tank's car. Chris placed the weed neatly into the Dutch, like a doctor performing surgery, and then licked and sealed it with just as must precision.

Chris had been smoking weed since he was about twelve years old; he and Brandon used to smoke together. All that changed when Brandon got accepted to college. All of sudden, he didn't want to hang out with Chris as much as he used to. Chris was upset at first, but he got over it, figuring Brandon was just doing what he needed to do to get out of the hood. In fact, he kind of respected him for it.

Chris opened the glove compartment of Tank's ride and searched around for a lighter. Once he found it, he lit the blunt, and took a long toke. He exhaled and passed it to Tank.

Chris was starting to unwind some. His heart had been beating fast ever since he left his mom's crib. Sitting back in his seat, he bobbed his head to the new Chamillionaire joint, "Ridin'."

Tank, also feeling the music, took two puffs from the blunt and then passed it back to Chris, who took another toke.

Chris was really feeling it now. The music and the blunt had put him in chill mode, and he was started to fade out. He passed the blunt back to Tank to finish off. He noticed that Tank rode right past the projects. "Where we going, man?" he asked, sitting up.

"I gotta make this run right quick." Tank pulled up next to this vacant lot on 19th and Montgomery Streets, opposite some abandoned, boarded-up houses.

Chris noticed a couple of smokers standing around waiting for Tank to serve them. He watched as Tank pulled out his product and exchanged with the fiends.

Walking back over to the car, Tank noticed his money wasn't right. One of the fiends had shorted him five dollars. This was the second time this dude tried to get him for his change.

Tank quickly turned back around and walked back over to the three smokers, who were now hovering in a circle in the process of fixing their high. "Where the fuck is the rest of money change?" he asked, his bottom lip quivering.

Tank pushed the tall thin female to the side causing her to fall on the ground. He stepped to the short, stocky gray-haired man who he knew shorted him of his change. Pulling the pistol from his pants, he aimed at his forehead.

"I-I-I'm sorry, man," the crackhead pleaded just as he was about to raise the pipe to his lips. "I'll have the rest of your money tomorrow."

Tank flipped the safety off the pistol and pulled the trigger, releasing a bullet in the crackhead's skull.

The smoker's body slumped to the ground, sending the crack pipe crashing down beside him, and the other two fiends scattered like roaches when they saw their partner's brains splattered at their feet.

Tank repositioned the safety on lock and stuffed the pistol back in pants. He strolled back to the car, got in, and pulled off. He doubled back to the projects, only four blocks down.

Chris sat tight and waited for the ride to be over. Tank had definitely blown his high. In enough trouble already, witnessing Tank's dirty work was just not in the cards.

Tank pulled up in front of the buildings and parked his car. Chris grabbed his bag from the back seat and followed Tank into the building, where they rode the elevator up to

Tank's fifth-floor apartment, located right across from the elevators.

When Chris came through the door, Brenda, Tank's mother, was laying on the couch in her bathrobe. She smiled at
Chris and continued watching her soaps.

"How you doing, Brenda?"

She gave Chris a long, seductive stare. "Damn, Chief! Every
time I see you, you look better and better."

Tank shot her the dirtiest look.

Shaking his head, Chris proceeded back to Tank's room.
He threw his bag on the floor and took a seat in the leather
lounger Tank had sitting in the corner by the window. He
pulled the lever on the side of the lounger, allowing him to
prop up his feet and get comfortable.

Chris saw a huge bag of weed on the TV stand, along with
a smaller bag filled with what looked like maybe two or three
kilos of coke. *Young bull is definitely eating well,* he thought. He
knew for a fact Tank was going to let him in on his business
endeavors. With the 50-inch flat-screen in the living room
and the 32-inch in the bedroom, money was definitely coming in.

He continued to survey the room. It had been a couple of
months since he was last at Tank's crib, and it looked nothing
like this. He had fifteen boxes of sneakers stacked neatly by
the closet door and a few pairs of "Trees" lined next to them.
Chris peeked in the closet next to him and saw five pair of
Evisu jeans, the tags still on them.

Tank disappeared from the room and returned with two
cold bottles of Corona. He handed one to Chris. Tank popped the top off the other and took a quick swig. He then
placed it on the dresser and walked back out of the room to
take a shower.

Chris popped the top of the beer and gulped it down in

less than two minutes. Beer really didn't do too much for him anymore. He'd been drinking too much hard liquor over the past few months. He wasn't satisfied with the buzz that the weed and the beer had given him, so he pulled an X pill out of his pocket and popped it. He sank down in the chair and closed his eyes.

Tank watched carefully from the doorway as Chris started to relax. He was hoping Chris popped a pill. That way he'd be so fucked up, he wouldn't be able to hold his own. All he had to do was wait it out. The pill would kick in, and Chris would be too fucked up to know what was going on. Tank was going to take Chris into the stairwell and put one in his head just like he did that smoker. Chris trusted him too much to think he would do such a thing, so Tank knew he wouldn't be expecting it.

Brandon was offering too much money for Tank to care about Chris or their friendship. Plus, Tank had a baby on the way by the chick down the hall. His cake had to be right if he wanted to move out of the projects when the baby was born.

Tank had plans for the money Brandon was offering; he was going to buy a crib up in West Oak Lane, somewhere in the white people neighborhood. He didn't want his kid growing up in the projects amidst gunfire like he did. As far as his momma was concerned, he would make sure her rent was always paid and that she had a couple dollars in her pocket.

Tank looked down at his diamond-encrusted Cartier wristwatch; it was just about eight in the evening. He went down the hall to the bathroom to take a shower.

Chris got up from the lounger and wandered into the living room where Tank's mother was still lying on the couch. He was so faded off the X he'd popped, he stood in front of her, dropped his pants to the floor, and pulled out his dick.

Brenda sat up from the couch and began stroking him off.

Swirling her wet tongue about his hardened dick, she finally planted her mouth around him. Chris's entire body tingled as she allowed the tip of his dick to touch her tonsils. Brenda was no stranger to Chris's dick. In fact, she was the first woman to introduce him to oral sex.

Brenda, now thirty-four, had Tank when she was fourteen, and Chris had been messing with her since he was a young bull, practically raising Tank. Back in the day, when Brenda was a recovering addict and she needed money, she would turn tricks, and Chris was her number one customer. And when Tank was old enough, Chris took him under his wing and put him on to the game. It had been years since they'd messed around, but for Chris, it felt like just yesterday.

Chris brushed the hair out of her face as she began deep-throating him. He held her head until he heard her gag. The hotness of her mouth drove Chris into pure insanity. He started thrusting his body back and forth into her mouth as fast as he could. She was beginning to gag again, but Chris was so into the heat of the moment, he just kept going.

Brenda tried to back away, but Chris grabbed her and continued ramming his dick into her mouth. He watched as her eyes bulged every time he forced himself into her; it was really turning him on.

Chris shoved himself into her one last time and pulled out, staining her lips with come, and Brenda wiped her face off with her bathrobe and lay back on the couch as if nothing happened.

Chris pulled his pants up and fastened them. He then dug into his pocket and pulled out a crisp hundred-dollar bill and threw it in her lap, like old times, and stumbled back into Tank's room.

Chris sat at the foot of Tank's bed and folded his hands. His eyesight was somewhat blurred, and his heart was beating so fast, he was starting to scare himself. The X pill he took had him buzzin' all crazy. He lay back on the bed and tried to allow his heart rate to slow down.

An annoying rumbling sound broke his concentration. He couldn't tell where it was coming from; it seemed muffled, so it was hard for him to track it down.

He jumped up from the bed and looked around the room. Finally, he realized it was coming from the TV stand. He reached over and grabbed the cell phone. He was going to throw it on the bed so he didn't have to hear the noise anymore, but he looked at the caller ID and saw Brandon's number.

He flipped the phone open. "Yo," he said, disguising his voice.

"That nigga dead yet?" Brandon asked, anxiously waiting for a response.

Chris closed the phone shut and placed it back on top of the television. His mind racing, he bent down and searched his bag for the Glock he'd stashed inside. He started to get nervous; it wasn't there.

"Looking for this?" Tank asked, holding the gun up for Chris to see. Smiling mischievously, Tank aimed at him and pretended to shoot.

Chris's eyes hardened in anger. He slid his hand in his boot and pulled out the switchblade he always kept for emergencies. His vision was still somewhat blurry, but it was coming back into focus real quick. He held it by his side and stood up.

Chris's first instinct was to charge him, but after what happened between him and Brandon, he decided that wouldn't be a good idea.

"I can't believe you going out like this," Chris said, walking slowly toward Tank.

"Nigga, please. Can you believe that I'm about to come up

a cool mil by laying you down?" Tank asked, his finger resting on the trigger.

"So after all the shit I did for you and ya mom, you gonna take me out just like that, huh?" Chris inched closer in Tank's direction.

"After all you did? Nigga, is you crazy? You call fucking my moms and giving her a couple of dollars here and there doing something?" Tank waved the gun in his face. "What you thought, I didn't know you was fucking my moms? Nigga, I should plant one right in ya head for that shit right there alone."

Chris's mouth tightened as his eyes zeroed in on Tank's. He noticed Tank's hand was trembling.

Tank aimed the gun at Chris's head and slowly squeezed down on the trigger, but Chris dove for the floor, and the bullet grazed the side of his temple, leaving a small half-inch tear in his flesh.

Chris jumped back up so fast, it startled Tank, who dropped the gun to the floor. He flicked open his switchblade and stabbed Tank in the upper chest. "Nigga, I raised your ass," he said, twisting the knife inside Tank.

"Fuck you!" Tank took his last bit of energy and spat in Chris's face.

"No, fuck you!" Chris took the knife out of Tank's lifeless body, allowing him to fall to the floor.

Tank's mother rushed down the hall. "What's going on in there?" It wasn't the first time she heard Tank let a shot off in the house, but it was the first time she had ever heard him and Chris argue.

"Nothing," Chris replied. "Go sit down somewhere."

Following his orders, she shuffled back down the hallway to the living room and laid back down on the couch.

Chris grabbed a T-shirt from the bedroom floor and wiped

the blood from his face. He then wrapped the T-shirt around his head and tied a knot in the back, He grabbed the Glock Tank had taken from him and stuffed it back in his bag. Then he grabbed the pound of weed and the two kilos of coke from the TV stand and placed them in his bag alongside the hand-gun.

After searching every inch of Tank's room, Chris came across an envelope of money taped to the bottom of the dress-er drawer. He placed the envelope in his bag with the rest of his belongings Chris started toward the bedroom door. He closed it behind himself and walked casually down the hall to the living room past Brenda, and out the front door.

When Brenda rushed back down the hallway and swung the door to Tank's room open wide, she noticed her son laid out on the side of the bed, his eyes rolled in the back of his head. She started to scream.

She ran after Chris who was now outside the apartment and in the main hallway. "You son of a bitch! What did you do to my son?"

"Didn't I tell your ass to go sit down somewhere?" Chris grabbed Brenda by the arm and pushed her back into the apartment.

He closed back the door to the apartment and headed for the stairwell. He took the bag down to the ground floor and out the side door. He placed his hood on his head and the bag on his back.

Chris strolled down the street without a care in the world, his hands in his pocket. He wasn't mad at Tank for trying to off him. In fact, he was impressed that he had enough heart to set him up. As for Brandon, it was already obvious as to what needed to be done. He'd broken every code that Chris lived by. Never in a million years did he think Brandon would put a price out on his head. It was time for Chris to show him who he was really fucking with.

# Chapter 3

## Homecoming
## Brandon

Brandon sat back in the rocking chair, holding his month-old baby. Kai was such a beautiful newborn; her curly jet-black mane complemented her coffee brown skin. Her hazel eyes reminded him of how beautiful her mother was. Mia had her dressed in a Winnie the Pooh sleeper to match the nursery theme. Brandon rocked back and forth as he fed her. He watched as her fat little jaws devoured the almost empty bottle. He then placed her over his shoulder and patted her lightly on the back.

Brandon really liked taking care of Kai; it was like she needed him more than anyone. He'd been home from the hospital for only two weeks, and since then, he had been taking care of the baby while Mia prepared herself to go back to work. Brandon's hospital bills really put a hurting on their bank account, and since he couldn't work, Mia had to.

After burping Kai, he placed her in the crib beside the rocking chair for her afternoon nap. He grabbed his cane and walked carefully across the hall to his and Mia's bedroom. He stood behind her at her vanity table and watched as she applied her makeup.

Mia applied her eyeliner with precision, creating a perfectly straight line. She then went on to apply her mascara. Brandon placed his hand on her shoulder in a loving manner; she was still just as pretty as she was the night they'd met. He often hated himself for being unfaithful. God knows he tried time and time again, but every time he made just a tiny bit of progress, some young pussy would approach him and he'd be back to square one.

Brandon hadn't been with anyone since he let Amy go, not even Mia. Every time he tried to make a move on her, she would act like she was too tired to have sex. He watched as she blotted her M•A•C Honeyflower lipstick with a tissue and applied her finishing powder. After eight months and three weeks of pregnancy, Mia was finally back in full swing. Having Kai left Mia with a bigger bustline and a fatter ass; her stomach was almost back to its original size, and her hair now flowed past her shoulders.

Mia patted his hand, which was resting on her shoulder, and he continued past her to the bed. He started to undress in hopes of getting some ass, but as soon as Mia saw him take off his pants, she got up from the vanity and went in the living room to grab her purse. She threw it across her shoulder and stood in the doorway of the bedroom.

Brandon was down to his boxer briefs when he noticed Mia standing quietly with her pocketbook on her shoulder and her keys dangling from her hand. "So where you headed now?" he asked, frowning.

"Oh, I have a meeting with my agent at one," she said casually, giving Brandon a vibe that she was telling a lie.

"So when will you be back?" he asked, trying to camouflage the annoyance in his voice.

"I don't know. I should be back before dinner. I'll give you a call to let you know," she said, turning to go out the door.

Mia had no sympathy for Brandon or his dick. Yes, she wanted to grab him and fuck the shit out of him, but her pride wouldn't allow it. He'd cheated on her once and she'd forgiven him, but this time, he could forget it. If it wasn't for the fact that Brandon's hospital bills put a strain on their finances, she would have left him and the baby and found herself another successful businessman.

She didn't want that damn baby anyway; Kai was just insurance in her eyes. She knew that if she got pregnant there was no way Brandon would get out of asking her to marry him. Plus, Kai was now the heir to Brandon's fortune. If anything was to happen to him, she would inherit all of his money and Mia would be the executor.

Mia had agreed to take on a few assignments until Brandon got back on his feet, and once he did, she was going to retire from modeling and just sit back and make him take care of her. After all, that was a man's job. Brandon was lucky to have a woman of Mia's stature; she could have easily left him when he'd cheated on her the first time, but in her mind, there was no way she was going to mold a man and then let another bitch come behind her and reap the benefits.

Mia almost forgot to tell him about the message she had taken for him while he was in the nursery with the baby this morning. She quickly turned back around. "I almost forgot to tell you. Lynn called," she said, allowing the words to roll out of her mouth through clenched teeth.

"A'ight, I'll see you later," he said in a rushed manner. He wanted to kick himself in the ass for sounding so eager for her to leave. Brandon didn't want to seem too interested in Lynn's call because he knew it would only upset Mia.

Watching as Mia left out the door, he grabbed the phone and dialed Lynn's number as soon as he heard the locks turn. He waited anxiously for her to answer, but received nothing but her answering machine.

Lynn was Brandon's young jawn. He'd met her on New Year's Day at the bar. He and Chris had just gotten into a huge fight over the record label and missing money, so he went to get his signature drink, gin on the rocks.

He ordered his drink and got a side of pussy to go with it. From that point on, he was hooked on her young, pretty ass.

Brandon started taking her personal, and next thing he knew, she called him saying she was pregnant. He cared about Lynn, but she didn't have the money Brandon needed to secure his future, so he had to put his feelings aside and marry Mia instead.

The excitement of talking to Lynn left him as soon as he heard the baby crying on the monitor. He grabbed his cane from the side of the bed and walked back across the hall to the nursery. He patted her softly on the back, and she went right back to sleep.

Brandon looked down at his Rolex watch; it was almost noon. The nanny would be arriving any minute now and he'd have the rest of his afternoon to himself.

He left the nursery and went into the living room to unlock the front door. He stood by the door for a moment, but when he noticed that the phone was ringing and he couldn't find the cordless, he left the living room area and went back to the bedroom to answer the call.

"Yeah," Brandon answered, frustrated that he had to walk all the way back to the bedroom to answer the phone.

"Hey," Lynn stuttered, twirling the phone cord around her finger. Her heart thudded when she'd heard his voice. She hadn't spoken with him in such a long time. She knew Mia would never tell him that she had been calling the hospital to see how he was doing. She'd sent him flowers every week with hopes of him seeing the notes attached to the bouquet, but still no response. Lynn kind of figured she had intercepted them also.

"Hey, so how's it going?" Brandon's tone softened. "When's the baby due?"

"Listen, I was wondering if we could get together and talk."

"Is everything okay?" Brandon said, sensing the concern in her voice.

The phone fell silent.

He sat back on the bed and waited for her response.

"I just need to speak to you in person is all."

"Look, I'll be over as soon as the nanny gets here."

"I'll see you then," she said, hanging up the phone.

Brandon placed the phone on the hook and turned his attention toward the doorway. His eyes almost bulged out of his head when he noticed Chris standing there with a clever grin on his face.

"Surprised to see me, huh?" Chris asked coolly, closing the door behind him and leaning against it.

Brandon eased the drawer to the bedside table open in hopes of grabbing his revolver.

Chris noticed and stuck his hand in his pocket allowing the imprint of his gun to show. "I wouldn't do that if I was you."

Brandon closed the drawer and placed his hands on his lap where Chris could see them.

Brandon wanted to shoot himself for leaving the door open. Chris was supposed to be dead by now anyway. He'd been calling Tank for a month now and he couldn't get in touch with him. He figured the job was done; something must have gone wrong if Chris was here in his bedroom.

"So what you going to do, huh? Kill me?" Brandon asked, not really wanting to know the answer.

"No, I'm not going to kill you . . . yet. I just wanted to show you how easy it is to touch you."

Chris opened the door to the bedroom and watched as the nanny walked past with the baby in her arms.

"It's a damn shame that baby of yours won't grow up to

know her father," Chris said, backing out of the bedroom door.

"Oh yeah? Do you really think you can kill me and get away with it?"

"Nigga, I can see you anytime I want. I'm just waiting it out. When I'm ready, I'ma put you down just like I did Tank." The corners of his mouth tightened. "Oh yeah, next time you decide to send someone for me, make sure they can do the job right." Chris continued to back down the hallway to the front door. Placing the hood to his sweatshirt on his head, he walked out as easily as he'd walked in.

Brandon grabbed the revolver from the bedside table drawer and his cane from the floor and followed behind him. By the time he made it to the front door of the condo, Chris was already gone. Brandon closed the door behind him and made sure all the locks were engaged.

Chris's threats burned in his mind as he walked back toward the bedroom. *Who does he think he is, coming up in my house like that, threatening my family?* Brandon was tired of Chris; he was becoming a pest.

Brandon placed the gun back in the drawer and grabbed his jacket from the closet. After what just happened with Chris, he really didn't want to leave the house, but he'd made Lynn a promise. He grabbed the keys to Mia's gray BMW coupe and headed for the elevators. He got halfway down the hall and decided to double back to the condo to grab the gun from the bedroom. With Chris on to the deal he made with Tank, he would rather be safe than sorry.

When Brandon arrived at his old apartment building, a chill ran up his spine. He walked through the marbled lobby and over to the front desk and requested the attendant to notify Lynn of his arrival. As he waited patiently for the attendant to ring her apartment, he began searching the lobby for familiar faces. He noticed Teresa, a big-bosomed redhead who lived down the hall from his old apartment. He'd had several trysts with her when her husband went out of town on business.

Brandon smiled at her, and she turned away in a huff. He didn't expect her to actually speak. Her husband had found out about their escapades after planting a camera in their bedroom, and divorced her shortly after, and she never spoke to him again.

Brandon heard the familiar clacking sound that he knew only Jimmy Choo's could make, and his head quickly jerked in the opposite direction. Only one woman could stride through the lobby like that, and it was none other than Natasha.

How could he ever forget about Natasha? She was the only other black resident in the building back then. She too had fallen prey to Brandon's good looks and mystical charm. He'd smiled at her once in the hallway, and the next night, they were butt naked in the laundry room. She loved a thrill, and Brandon was always able to give her just that.

He flashed his pearly white teeth and gave her a friendly wave. She smiled at him and continued out the door. *Natasha is one bad female*, he thought.

"You can go on up," the attendant said, interrupting Brandon's thoughts.

"Thanks." Brandon headed over to the elevators.

Once on board, he began replaying in his mind the last time he'd seen Lynn. It was nearly six months ago when he told her he was engaged. In fact, it was one of the hardest things he'd ever done in his life. Lynn was so much more than just a fuck for him. It was just that he needed money, something she wasn't able to provide. He often wished that Lynn was the one he'd married. At least she could cook.

Brandon knocked lightly on the door. Standing there waiting for her to answer, his palms began to sweat. He couldn't believe he was so nervous about seeing her. He held his breath when he heard the lock turn.

The door swung open, and he came face to face with Lynn. He noticed almost instantly that her belly was just as flat as the first day they'd met. Reaching out to Lynn's middle section, he couldn't believe his eyes.

"Excuse you," she said, rolling her eyes and walking into the apartment.

"My fault." Brandon placed his hand in his pocket and walked in behind her. *Same old Lynn*, he thought as he placed the lock on the door.

Something was definitely wrong. Lynn should be delivering next month, and yet the gigantic stomach he hoped to see wasn't there.

Brandon took a seat on the couch and rested his cane on the floor beside him. He glanced around the room and frowned. The walls that once held his expensive, one-of-a-kind artwork were now bare, and painted a drab color of olive. Realizing he was just a visitor and that he'd given Lynn the apartment to do as she liked, he decided to keep quiet about his belongings.

He focused his attention toward Lynn, who had taken a seat across from him in a chair. "So what's up?" he asked, folding his hands in his lap.

Lynn sat up toward the edge of the chair. "I lost our son last month." She got up from the chair and walked over to the window. Her eyes were tearing, and she didn't want Brandon to see her break down.

She stared out to the park and watched as a mother grabbed her son from the swing and swung him around before placing him in his stroller. Watching someone else interacting with their child only made her feel more uneasy. "They said the miscarriage was due to my diabetes," she said, wrapping her arms around herself.

Lynn lowered her head. She was really looking forward to being a mother. There wasn't a day that went by that she didn't think about her baby. She often felt as if God had punished her for being with a man who was practically married. She continued to stare out of the window.

Brandon grabbed his cane from beside the couch and made his way over to the window where Lynn was standing. He reached out almost hesitantly and placed his hand on her shoulder. "Everything's going to be all right." He pulled Lynn closer to him.

Lynn turned around and laid her face in his warm chest. Her dampened face left wet spots on Brandon's crisp Armani button-down shirt.

Brandon didn't care though; he just wanted to make sure she was all right. But one thing bothered him. "Why didn't you call me when you were in the hospital?" he asked, patting her on the back.

"I did call you." She looked up into his eyes. "I left like a hundred messages with your wife."

Brandon kissed her on the forehead and held her closely. Anger rose inside of him. Mia had been hiding his messages from him. If she did that, then he knew she was capable of much more. Allowing all thoughts of Mia to move to the back of his mind, he focused on consoling Lynn.

"Come on and sit on the couch," he said, leading her away from the window.

Lynn followed him over and sat beside him. She wiped her face with the sleeve of her T-shirt and sat quietly. The look

Brandon had given her when she mentioned the countless messages she left with his wife made her realize that he wasn't just blowing her off. In her heart, she knew Brandon wasn't that coldhearted. Sure, they didn't have the best relationship after she'd found out about his engagement, but they were at least cordial toward each other.

Lynn sighed. "Well, I guess you can leave now. It's really no need for you to be here, since I'm not pregnant and all."

Brandon looked at her as if she had bumped her head. He could be a son of a bitch, and he knew that, but he wouldn't leave her when she needed him the most. "Naw, I'ma stick around for a little while. I wanna make sure everything is good with you before I leave."

"You sure about that? What about your wife?"

"What about her?" Brandon said pulling Lynn closer to him allowing her to rest her head back on his chest.

Lying quietly against Brandon's chest, Lynn listened to the rhythm of his heartbeat. Something about being with Brandon soothed her soul and made her feel safe. Lynn still had feelings for Brandon, and even though she would most likely never tell him, she just needed to enjoy him being there with her at that very moment.

That low-down conniving wife of his was really beginning to bother her. *She is such a bitch,* Lynn thought. She'd explained the situation to her when she'd called Brandon. Mia knew there was a chance that Lynn would miscarry, and yet she wasn't a decent enough woman to let Brandon know. If they ever crossed paths, Lynn was going to dig in her ass. She often wondered what was so special about her that made Brandon settle down, and what she looked like. Was she prettier than Lynn, or more sophisticated?

Brandon looked over to the end table beside him and picked up the remote. He flicked on the TV to ESPN's *SportsCen-*

*ter* and propped his feet up on the coffee table. He looked over at the clock on the cable box. It was going on two thirty in the afternoon. One thing was sure. He had no plans on going home anytime soon. *Let Mia wait*, he thought. *She made me wait for my messages.*

"Where the fuck is he?" Mia said rambling out loud. She was sipping on her third glass of Merlot. She took one last mouthful and slammed the glass in the sink, causing it to break.

The baby was crying, and the nanny had left well over three hours ago.

Mia yelled at the baby from the kitchen. "Shut up! Damn!"

Looking over at the clock on the mantel, she noticed it was just turning ten fifteen. She called his phone thirty-six times, and it went straight to voicemail. Something told her he was up to no good.

Busting in the bedroom in a fury, Mia sifted through Brandon's closet and dresser drawers and found nothing but old cleaner receipts and hotel matchbooks. She was trying to concentrate, but the baby's cries were starting to sting her ears. Her silk green La Perla dressing gown flung open as she hurried into the nursery to pick the baby up.

After patting Kai on the back for a few minutes, she finally calmed down. Mia placed her back into the crib and continued on her rampage, searching all of his drawers and closets.

The only other place to look was the nightstand. She sat down on Brandon's side of the bed and allowed the satin comforter to caress her bare legs. She opened the nightstand drawer and saw nothing but papers. She noticed a large manila envelope that with the word *confidential* in big red letters. She grabbed the envelope from the drawer and opened it up.

After reading the first page, her mouth dropped to the floor. She continued reading the consultation from the lawyer. According to the paperwork, Brandon had sold the label for three million dollars. She'd just checked his account yesterday, and there was only $250,000 available.

Mia threw the envelope and the rest of its contents against the bedroom wall. *He must have a secret account,* she thought. She lay across the bed on her back and fondled the comforter between her fingers. *How could he sell the label without telling me?*

Brandon had mentioned closing the Philadelphia office, but he didn't say anything about the New York location. She got off the bed and picked the envelope up from the floor. *It all makes perfectly good sense now. Chris is trying to kill Brandon over the money from selling the label.* If she'd known that, she might have tried to help him. Chris was an asshole, but right is right, and he deserved his cut of the money.

Mia started to feel faint; they were close to broke. After paying off Brandon's hospital bills, Mia's account was worse off than it had ever been; she was down to her last million. She just knew he was going to take care of her for the rest of her days but how could he? They were two months away from the soup kitchen line.

The thought of her going back to living a mediocre life flashed before her eyes, and she was back at her tiny apartment in the heart of West Philly. She could smell the disgusting odor of fried fish and malt liquor. She'd fought so hard to provide for herself, there was no way she was going back there.

Brandon thought she'd come from a well-off family and had no idea she was an orphan who grew up in multiple foster homes, and was molested by every man who could get their hands on her.

When she'd met her ex-fiancé, it was like a breath a fresh air. Mia rode that gravy train right out of her one-bedroom into a six-bedroom mini-mansion with a convertible BMW in the driveway. With a little manipulation and a vicious head game, she was able to finagle out of him his modeling contacts and an unbelievable amount of cash. If Brandon thought he was going to take that away from her, he had another think coming.

Mia searched through the rest of the papers. Irritated, she threw the papers to the floor, and out came the ultrasound picture of Lynn's baby. That was it. She'd had enough.

She picked the ultrasound picture up from the floor and gripped it tightly in her hand. She hurried out of the bedroom and into the kitchen where she left her purse. She grabbed her wallet and searched for the card to the investigator she had follow Brandon before they were formally introduced. With the ultrasound picture still firmly in hand, she dialed the number on the card.

"Detective Montgomery," a husky voice answered.

"Yes, I need some information about someone." Mia looked down at the ultrasound picture. It was time for her to find out a little bit more about this Lynn Whitmore. She needed a face to go with the name and possibly an address. Brandon had no idea who he was fucking with. If it was game he wanted, then it was game he was going to get.

And Mia had no intentions of playing clean. Just like her sex game, she always played dirty.

# Chapter 4

### Robbing Cradles
### Chris

"Aww shit!" Chris howled, trying to concentrate on his nut. "Damn! You got some good ass!"

A tingling sensation ran through Chris's body as he released himself into the condom. He gave off one last pump and pulled out slowly, making sure the rubber was still intact. He peeled the condom off and dropped it on the floor beside the bed. He then rolled over on his back and rested his head on the plush pillows behind him. He wiped the sweat from his brow and stared at the ceiling.

Ever since Chris stopped popping pills two months ago, the only other feeling that could come anywhere close to that high was sex. After Tank had tried to take him out, Chris decided that he needed to be alert at all times. He'd even stopped smoking weed. His weakness now lied in a young piece of ass.

He looked over at Shawn, who'd just returned from the bathroom. Chris was beginning to get aroused again as he watched the muscles in Shawn's back flex as he sat on the side of the bed and pulled a T-shirt over his head.

Chris grabbed his arm and yanked him in his direction, but Shawn snatched away in a huff and continued dressing.

Chris sat up on the bed. "What the hell is wrong with you?"

"Nothing," Shawn responded, placing his right boot on and lacing it up.

Chris grabbed at his arm again, only for Shawn to pull away once more.

"Look, man, I'ma ask you one more time." Chris rose to his feet and stood in front of him. "What the fuck is your problem?"

Shawn rolled his eyes at Chris and then folded his arms in front of his well-defined chest. "You told me you was going to take me shopping last week and you ain't even remember."

Chris raised an eyebrow. "Is this what ya little attitude is about?"

"What you think?" Shawn sucked his teeth and went back to lacing up his boots.

Chris shook his head in disbelief. He went over to his jacket pocket and pulled out five crisp hundred-dollar bills and threw them on the bed beside him. "Fix ya face," Chris told him. "I'm tired of you acting like a bitch when you don't get ya way." He eased back down on the bed and settled his head slowly back upon the pillows.

Shawn sneered. "Well, you shouldn't make promises you ain't gonna keep." He snatched the money off the bed and stuffed it into his uniform pants. He then grabbed his school bag from the closet located right next to his side of the bed, and placed it on his back. "So are you gonna drop me off at school or what?" he asked, shuffling toward the door of Chris's tiny boarding room.

Chris looked down at his naked body and then back up at Shawn. "Do I look like I'm dropping you off at school?" Chris yawned, and closed his eyes shortly thereafter.

"Fuck it. I'll just walk then." Shawn slammed the door behind him.

Chris could hear Shawn stomping down all three flights of his boarding house and out the door. *If he only knew,* Chris thought. *If Shawn had played his cards right, he could've gotten bro-*

*ken off with way more than a measly five hundred. That's the problem with young bulls—They see a little money and they get caught up.*

Chris was really starting to feel Shawn. He'd never latched on to someone as quickly as he did with him. He'd met Shawn one day last month at the Chinese store on the avenue, not too far from his house. When Chris walked in the store to buy a loosie, he ran right smack into Shawn, spilling his chicken wing and fried rice platter on the sidewalk. Annoyed at wearing half of his platter on the front of shirt, Shawn demanded Chris to buy him another.

Chris loved when a nigga had enough heart to step to him like that, especially a young bull. So he dug into his pocket, placed a fifty in his hand and told him to keep the change. But when Chris went to grab his hand back Shawn neglected to let go.

At first, Chris was going to punch him dead in the mouth, but when he noticed the look Shawn had in his eyes, he knew what the deal was. Chris forgot all about what he came to the store for.

Next thing he knew, he was back at the boarding house where he stayed, butt-ass naked, getting his balls sucked by this young bull. After several rounds of heated sex, things finally calmed down, and Chris was able to ask his name. And they spent the rest of the night talking and getting to know one another.

It wasn't until two weeks ago that he found out that Shawn was only eighteen, and that was because it was his birthday. That's the reason why he was so pissed off at Chris about the shopping trip he'd promised him. It wasn't that Chris didn't want to break bread with the young bull; he was just preoccupied with more important things.

***

With Tank gone, Chris was able to reclaim his spot and run the projects. It was never said who offed Tank, but niggas around the way knew and respected Chris for laying him down. Plus, running a new team of niggas was a lot of work. He had to make sure business was running smoothly and that none of his young bulls was trying to burn him for cash. Chris knew that as soon as he let his guard down, a nigga would fuck up, and he would have to clean up the mess. So he kept a close eye on all his workers, and he trusted no one.

That brought Chris back to his plans for Brandon. He wasn't too concerned about him at the moment because he knew Brandon didn't hold enough weight in the hood to find another soldier in the streets like Tank, or had enough cash to hire one.

Chris ran into Sam, Mia's homegirl, at an underground party Shawn had dragged him to last night. He was actually surprised to see her there. He should have known she was into women too because she would always talk about how gorgeous Mia's body was. Sam told him that Mia was running through money like crazy and that she and Brandon were close to filing for bankruptcy. She was so drunk, she'd even mentioned that Mia had found herself a little playmate of her own.

It was only a matter of time until Brandon would be desperate for a couple dollars and Chris knew that out of desperation, a nigga would be willing to do almost anything. He was going to set Brandon up on the block and make him work for his money. And he wasn't talking about selling drugs—He was thinking more like selling ass. That way, Chris could be his number one customer. Seeing Brandon get fucked in the ass would be more satisfying than putting a bullet in his head. He'd feel like he lost his manhood over and over again each time he had to bend over.

Chris was now back to being one of the most feared niggas in North Philly. With the money he brought in on the weekly basis, he had already stacked close to a quarter of a million dollars. He'd even paid the "poppy" store back for the twenty grand he robbed them, and added an extra ten grand for them to drop the case. Things were starting to look up for him.

Chris placed the covers over his head to shield his face from the rays of sun bursting through the window.

Just as he nodded off, his cell phone rang. He reached his arm from under the covers and felt around on the nightstand for the phone. He pulled it under the covers with him and pressed the talk button. "Hello," he said, yawning into the phone.

"Hey," a sweet yet mellow voice responded on the other end.

Chris pulled the covers from over his head and sat up in the bed. Tracy's voice echoed in his ears as he tried to gather himself for what to say next. It had been at least six months since he'd heard from her.

"What's up, baby? How's my young bull?"

Tracy smiled at the sound of him calling her *baby*. "He's fine," she said, stalling on what she really called about. "We need to meet up."

"Meet me at the spot in an hour." Chris got up and walked over to the closet to grab a thermal shirt from the clean clothes he had sitting on the floor in a trash bag.

"Okay, I'll be there," she said him and hung up the phone.

Chris put his dark denim True Religion jeans on and laced up a pair of fresh Timb boots. He then grabbed his hammer from the nightstand table and tucked it in the back of his pants. He scanned the room one last time to make sure he wasn't forgetting anything. He turned the TV off, snatched his rhinestone Ed Hardy punk hoodie from the chair, and locked the door to his room.

He proceeded down the hallway and into the stairwell of his building. When he got down to the first floor, he noticed Shawn standing in front of the building talking to some dude who seemed to be around the same age as Chris.

Sneaking up behind him, Chris gripped him by the forearm and yanked him away from the conversation without a second thought. "What the fuck is you doing?" he asked, pushing him back into the building and closing the door behind him. "I thought you were going to school?"

"Get the fuck off of me!" Shawn tried to pull himself away from Chris's strong embrace.

Chris's forehead wrinkled, and his faced turned a deep red. He gripped Shawn up by his uniform collar and yanked him so close, Shawn could fell the hotness of Chris breath on his face.

"You think it's cute to be in another nigga's face, huh?" Chris said, pulling him in closer.

Shawn swallowed the gulp in his throat. "He's just a friend."

"Bullshit!" Chris shot back. "The next time I see you in another man's face, you gonna have a problem on your hands." He loosened his grasp slightly when he noticed the fear in Shawn's face. "This is what I want you to do. March your little ass upstairs and wait for me to come back." He let go of him, causing him to stumble backward and fall to the floor.

Shawn sat on the floor by the mailboxes and grasped for air. He massaged his pulsating neck. He got up and started up the stairs to the room. Realizing Chris was on his way out, he turned around and stopped at the top of the first flight of stairs. "Where you going anyway?"

"Don't worry about where I'm going. Just do as I said." Chris turned to go out of the door to the building.

He looked down at the clock on his cell phone; it was a little past ten thirty in the morning. Twenty minutes had already passed since he'd talked to Tracy. If he didn't hurry, he was going to be late, and he didn't want to give her the impression that he was blowing her off.

Chris stood in the vestibule and waited for Shawn to follow his instructions, tapping his foot impatiently. Shawn was really starting to press his luck. Trying to control his temper, he started toward the stairs after him.

When Shawn saw Chris coming, he nodded and continued up the stairs to Chris's room.

At first, Shawn had liked the idea of being with Chris, but lately, he was becoming too possessive. He wasn't about to confront Chris about his ways, knowing that the only way to keep him happy was to fuck him like a porn star. Shawn had no problem doing that, as long as Chris was willing to give him porn star money to perform.


Chris's mind wandered as he drove down to the stables to meet Tracy. After all of the time they spent as a couple, she still knew their meeting spot. Whenever Chris was in trouble with the law, he always told Tracy to meet him down at the old horse stables on 32nd Street.

No matter where she was in the city, she always managed to beat him there. There was no doubt that Chris still cared about Tracy. He just wasn't sure how she felt about him.

Cheating on her was one of the biggest mistakes he'd ever made in his life. He would do anything to have his family back, but he knew that would never happen. Tracy was now married, and from what his mother told him, very much in love. He still couldn't understand how she could up and marry a man she hadn't even dated for more than six months. Chris felt like Tracy got married to hurt him, and that, it did. The thought of his son calling another man daddy enraged him.

Chris pulled up to the stables and parked behind Tracy's gold CLK55. He got out of his little beat-up Pontiac Grand Prix and leaned against it.

Tracy emerged from the car wearing a pair of wide-framed Christian Dior glasses that took up half of her face. They were so dark, she could hardly see out of them. Her hair was slicked back in a long, weaved ponytail that extended to the back of her nape. She grabbed her Gucci clutch, keys from the car, and gently closed the door.

As she walked toward Chris, her mind started to race. *Was she really ready to see him? Did he still have feelings for her like she did for him?* Tracy stood in front of him and placed her hand on her hip in a sassy manner. "It took you long enough to get here."

*Same old Tracy,* Chris thought. *Still a wise ass, and as gorgeous as the day she left me.* "So what's up?" he asked, trying to play it cool and not undress her with his eyes. The Seven jeans she had on fit like a glove, and her brandy-colored mink jacket only made her look even more hot. Chris would give anything to slide up in between those sweet thighs again. Out of all his lovers, Tracy was definitely the best, always concerned about his needs in the bedroom and performing accordingly. She rarely ever cared if she got her shit off, and was just happy to be able to keep him satisfied.

"I need a huge favor."

"A favor, huh. What type of favor we talking?"

"If you would let me finish without jumping in, I could tell you." Tracy took a deep breath. "Look, I need to borrow a couple dollars."

"How much you need?" Chris asked, digging into his pocket. "That nigga of yours ain't fitting the bill, huh. It's cool. I got you."

Chris was amused at the thought of Tracy's new man not being able to provide for her. Tracy had expensive taste and was used to getting at least five grand from Chris a month to go shopping for herself.

Tracy's car keys slipped from her hand and fell into the dirt beside her. When she bent down to pick them up, her sunglasses fell off her face and onto the ground too. She quickly picked them up and placed them back on her face, hoping that Chris wasn't paying any attention. When she stood up, Chris snatched the glasses right off her face before she could even say a word. He threw them back to the ground and smashed them with his boot, crumbling them to scattered pieces of useless plastic and metal.

"What the fuck happened to your face?" Chris leaned in to touch her bruised black-and-blue cheek.

She swatted his hand away and backed up. "Nothing. I fell."

"Please tell me that nigga ain't hitting on you." Chris pounded his fist against the hood of the car.

Chris's eyes welled up. He turned around and wiped them before Tracy caught on to what was going on. Tracy had been through enough pain in her life when they were together, and there was no way he was going to allow someone else to hurt her.

"Look, I just need some money so I can get me and Li'l Chris a place," she said, staring down at the ground.

Chris lifted her chin up and kissed her softly on the lips. He then placed a wad of fifties and hundreds in her hand.

Tracy stood frozen as she just realized what had happened. Chris's soft lips sent chills through her aching body. Hakeem, her husband, had whipped her badly last night, almost to the point where she couldn't walk, all because she didn't wash the dinner dishes. After cooking a four-course meal and putting Little Chris to bed, she was exhausted. This wasn't the first time he'd beat her. In fact, it was the hundred and thirty-seventh time he'd put his hands on her, according to Tracy's count.

Chris's stomach tightened. He just had to ask her about his son. He took a seat on the hood of the car. "Did he hit my young bull?"

"No, he ain't never put his hands on Li'l Chris," she said, placing the wad of cash in her jacket pocket. "He takes all of his anger out on me."

"I swear to God, I'll kill that nigga if he hits you again." Chris' eyebrows pointed inward.

"I'll pay you back as soon as I can," she said, walking back toward her car.

Before she could open the door, a tinted-out BMW 3 Series rolled up and parked beside her car. Tracy's first instinct told her to run, but Hakeem got out of the car so fast on her, she felt like a little schoolgirl who just got caught by her father.

Chris remained seated on the hood of his car, trying his best to remain calm. After seeing what he did to Tracy's face, he was itching to give him a beating.

"What? You think I ain't know where you was going?" Hakeem yanked Tracy by the arm so hard, he almost dislocated her shoulder. "You can't make a phone call in my house without me knowing about it."

"I-I-I was just—"

"You little sneaky bitch," he said, shaking her with all his strength. He then smacked her in the face. "I told you I didn't want you talking to this nigga. You out here putting my business out in the streets?"

Tracy held her face, which was now stinging.

"Whoa, homie!" Chris jumped off the hood of his car on to the ground. "What the fuck is ya problem?"

"Nigga, you need to mind ya business." Hakeem let go of Tracy and met Chris face to face.

"Nigga, she *is* my business," Chris puffed his chest up against Hakeem's, who was a good four inches taller than him.

"I'm your son's daddy now, nigga. You just some washed up dude that couldn't keep his bitch happy," Hakeem said, pointing his finger in Chris's face.

Hakeem's words cut like a sharp blade. Chris hadn't seen his son in a while, but it wasn't a day that went by that he didn't think about him or Tracy.

Chris pulled his .45 from his belt and aimed it at Hakeem's chest. He bit his bottom lip as he eased the safety off lock.

"Oh yeah, so you my son's daddy, huh? Nigga, you must be out of ya mind coming at me like that. This is what we're going to do. Tracy's going to get in her car and ride off. Nigga, I don't even want her to witness what I'm about to do to you," Chris said, his finger firmly on the trigger.

"Chris, please don't hurt him." Tracy eased herself in front of Hakeem and the gun.

*She must be losing her mind.* Chris just knew Tracy was too smart to be with an asshole like Hakeem. It just struck him that he didn't even know where she'd met the bull. "Tracy, move out the way," he said, lowering the gun to his side.

"Please, just go. I'll call you later."

"Naw, let this nigga ride off first. At least I'll know you all right."

"Fuck that! I ain't going nowhere."

Tracy turned toward Hakeem. "Baby, please just go. Let me take care of this. I'll meet you back at the house."

Hakeem eyed Chris down, a smug look on his face. "Fine, but you better be there by noon." He looked down at his Movado watch. It was eleven o'clock.

Hakeem walked over to his car and opened the door. He took one last look at Chris and then said, "It's cool, nigga. I'm going to see you."

"I hope that's a promise," Chris said, pointing the gun in his direction.

Hakeem nodded and got back into his car and drove off in a hurry, leaving clouds of dust behind.

Chris placed the .45 back in the holster on his pants. "Are you really going to go back to that nigga?"

"I don't know, Chris. I just don't know. He's all I got."

"You got me," Chris blurted out. "I know I'm a son of a bitch, but I ain't never put my hands on you."

Chris had finally said the words she wanted to hear. The only problem was, she could never get past the fact that he slept with a man. Every time it crossed her mind, she wanted to vomit. Chris was the only man she'd ever loved. She liked Hakeem and hoped that she could love him as much as she loved Chris.

"Where did you meet that nigga at anyway?"

Chris had definitely seen him before, but he just couldn't place him. He knew for sure that he wasn't from around the way.

"He's from New York. He has family out here."

"All I know is, if I see your face like that again, I'ma lay that nigga out. So you make sure he stays in his place from now on," Chris said, walking over to his car. "And take care of my son. I want to see him this weekend." Chris started his car. "Meet me at my mom's crib for Sunday dinner."

Strutting over to her car, Tracy said, "I'll see you then."

Chris pulled off and made his way back over to the boarding house. He parked out front and sat there with the car running. He really didn't feel like being bothered with Shawn right now. Seeing Tracy made him realize everything he was missing in his life. Yeah, he had money, and yeah, he was well respected, but nothing could ever measure up to him having his family back.

It was five p.m. on Sunday evening, and Tracy and Li'l Chris had yet to arrive. Chris paced back and forth in the living room, occasionally stopping to look out of the window to see if Tracy's gold CLK 55 pulled up. He tried not to worry, but he couldn't help himself. He called her cell phone once more, but it just rang until the answering machine picked up.

Chris's mother sat patiently at the dining room table, which was set with her finest china. She too was looking forward to seeing Tracy and Li'l Chris. Since Tracy had started dating her new man, Ms. Ruth hardly ever saw her or her grandson. There used to be a time when she had to practically kick Tracy out of her house.

Tracy had brought her new man over for dinner one evening, and Ms. Ruth picked up a bad vibe about him. He seemed to be scoping her place out. He'd asked to use the bathroom, and after twenty minutes, Ms. Ruth got a little suspicious and went upstairs to check on him. When she reached the top of the steps, she noticed the door to Chris's old bedroom was cracked. She opened the door and found him sifting through the dresser drawers. He claimed he was looking for a hand towel to dry off, but Ms. Ruth knew better. That day she told Tracy that he was no longer welcome at her house, and that was the last time she had Tracy or her grandson over for dinner. Hakeem told her, if he wasn't invited, then neither was Tracy.

Chris ran to the door when he saw Tracy's car back into the driveway. He sighed with relief and rushed out to meet his son at the front steps. He sat on the front steps and waited for

Tracy to unstrap Li'l Chris from his car seat. When she placed him on the ground, he waddled over to Chris with a look of confusion on his face.

Chris held out his hands. "Come here, little man."

Li'l Chris ran back over to Tracy and grabbed her leg. He hid behind her and started to whine. "Mommy, I go home. I want my daddy," he repeated several times.

Chris lowered his arms in devastation. His own son didn't know who he was anymore. Chris sat on the steps and watched as Tracy hoisted him up onto her hip and locked the doors to her car. Li'l Chris placed his head on her shoulder and whimpered, repeating the same words over again. Tracy patted him on the back and walked up the steps to the house.

Chris had waited all week to see his son, practically buying every toy he could find for a three-year-old.

"I'm sorry he's acting like this. It's just he hasn't seen you in so long that he probably don't remember who you are."

"He really call that nigga *Daddy*?" Chris asked, still sitting on the steps.

"Yeah." Tracy opened the screen door to the house and took Li'l Chris inside.

Ms. Ruth met her at the door and took Li'l Chris into her arms without hesitation. She kissed Tracy on the cheek and tried to act as if she didn't notice the bruise, which seemed to be healing, below Tracy's eye.

Chris sat on the steps for at least half an hour; his body just wouldn't budge. He never thought he would see the day his son called another man daddy.

# Chapter 5

### Strapped for Cash
### Brandon

"This can't be right," Brandon said in his most stern voice. "I demand to speak to your supervisor."

"No problem, sir. I'll get him right away." The teller left the window and disappeared into a nearby room behind the counter.

He stood at the teller window on his cane and waited for the manager to arrive. There was no way his bank account only had $75,000 in it. He checked it last week and there was well over $250,000 grand available. He knew it had to be a mistake. *Maybe the teller punched in the wrong account number. Yeah, that had to be it.*

"Can I help you, sir?" a tall light-skinned man in a navy blue polo shirt and tan khakis asked.

Brandon cleared his throat. "Yes, I was telling your clerk here that there must be some sort of mistake. There's no way I only have seventy-five thousand dollars in my account." Realizing his voice had risen a good ten decibels, he looked over his shoulder to see who was behind him and saw an older woman who looked as if she needed a hearing aid, and a young girl who seemed preoccupied with texting on her cell phone. He turned back around in just enough time to see the teller whisper something into the manager's ear and point at the screen.

The manager looked at the screen and nodded at the teller. "Mr. Brunson, please step into my office, so we can go over your transactions." The manager ushered him over toward the back of the bank.

Brandon followed behind him and took a seat in one of the two leather chairs that sat in his cramped office. There was a huge stack of papers and files covering the left side of his desk and a potted plant and a picture frame of two male children who looked to be twins on the other. Brandon placed his cane on the floor beside him and leaned forward to rest his forearms on the manager's desk.

The manager quickly seated himself behind his computer and started typing up Brandon's account information. He turned the screen toward Brandon and allowed him to see several big-ticket purchases totaling over $150,000 made with his bank card at Bloomingdale's, Barneys, and Bergdorf Goodman, the three *B*'s, as Mia referred to them.

Brandon loosened the tie around his neck. *How could she be so careless?* He'd told her that money was a little tight. "Can I get a printout of those transactions?" Brandon said, still looking at the computer screen in disbelief. What bothered him the most was, he didn't recall seeing her bring any packages in the house.

"You sure can."

Brandon grabbed the lengthy printout from the manager, folded it in half, and placed it under his arm as if it was a newspaper. He then grabbed his cane from the floor and rose from his seat. "Thank you for your time," he said, grabbing the knob to the office door.

"Mr. Brunson, you may want to make sure that your wife is keeping you abreast of her purchases. You know that once you're below one hundred thousand dollars, we have to switch you to a lower interest account." The manager turned the screen back toward him.

Brandon nodded and proceeded out the door. Ignoring everyone and everything as he walked through the bank, he shuffled over to his car and got in. He took his loosened tie all the way off and threw it in the back seat. He then unbuttoned the top three buttons of his Burberry dress shirt and tried to wind down.

He just couldn't understand for the life of him what was making Mia act like this. She was spending more and more time out in the streets and less time at home with him and the baby. It was like she didn't want to be bothered with him or Kai. He took her excuse of not wanting to have sex because she was still healing from the baby, but her spending thousands of dollars behind his back was just unacceptable.

As Brandon drove down the street to his house, he rehearsed the conversation that needed to take place between him and Mia. He was going to go in there and demand that she not only tell him what she did with all that money but also why she had been acting so strange. Things weren't going as Brandon planned. He was supposed to be living on her, not the other way around. Plus, Mia had taken on several modeling assignments, so there was no reason for her to tap into his account, since she had her own money.

Pulling into the building's parking lot, Brandon noticed a brand-new 2007 Maserati Quattroporte Sport GT parked in the designated space marked for his apartment. He parked his car beside the cherry red Maserati and got out to take a look. Brandon peeped in the window of the car and admired the plush tan leather bucket seats and alloy pedals.

In his mind, Brandon knew Mia had purchased that car, but he just didn't want to believe it. He backed away from the window and walked around to the back of the car to look at the tag, which read 1SEXYB. He was just about to boil over. Not only did she go on a massive shopping spree, she'd just purchased a car for $120,000.

He hurried over to the elevator and waited for it to arrive. When he got to the door of the apartment, he took a deep breath and slid his key card through the door. To his surprise, the house was silent, meaning both Mia and the baby were most likely still asleep. Brandon took his suit jacket off and threw it across the love seat. He walked back to the nursery to check on the baby and just as he thought, she was sound asleep. He kissed her on the forehead and carefully closed the door behind him, making sure not to wake her.

He then made his way across the hall to the bedroom. Hearing muffled sounds coming from the room as he approached the door, he cracked it slightly and there was Mia sitting up in the bed talking on the phone. From what Brandon could see, she seemed to be deep into her conversation. He pushed the door wide open and stood in the doorway.

Startled to see him, Mia clicked the off button on the cordless without saying bye to the person on the other end. "So when did you get back?" she asked, placing the phone back on the cradle on the bedside table.

"I just got in." Brandon took a seat on the oak bench that sat at the foot of the bed. "So who was that on the phone?"

"Oh, just my mother." Mia flashed a fake smile. "We're supposed to get together for lunch today."

"So why did you hang up so fast when I came in the room?" he questioned, searching her face for signs that she was lying.

"No reason. We finished our conversation." Mia said, without flinching. She got up from the bed and began digging in her armoire closet. She returned from the closet with her terry cloth Victoria's Secret bathrobe.

Brandon continued to sit at the edge of the bed on the oak bench and watched as she passed by him and made her way to the bathroom.

Mia sat on the side of the tub and turned on the water.

"So what do you have planned for today?" she asked, trying to make small talk.

Mia looked over at him as he stood now frozen in the middle of the bedroom floor. She could really care less what Brandon had planned today or any day. She was just trying to be civil until she bled him dry for every penny he owned. Once the money was gone, so was she. Mia knew that Brandon most likely had several bank accounts in which he kept money that she had no idea about. He was just sneaky like that. She had access to the one of the accounts and planned on finding the others with the help of the detective she'd hired.

She held her hand under the faucet to test the temperature. Once it was warm enough, she plugged the tub and poured in a handful of Carol's Daughter Jamaican Punch Body Aches Bath Salts. Then she dropped her bathrobe and negligee to the floor and submerged herself in the warm water.

"I went to the bank today, and I noticed there was a hefty amount of money missing from my account."

"Oh, I forgot to tell you about that," Mia said, settling herself into the bathtub.

"What the fuck do you mean, you forgot to tell me that?"

Mia grabbed her loofa sponge from the bath tray. "I use your account all the time. So what's the problem?"

"The problem is that you took one hundred fifty grand out of my account." He folded his arms across his chest. "Where the hell do you get off doing that?"

"I see you helped yourself to a shopping spree at your favorite stores. And that fucking car . . . where do you get off going out and buying an expensive car without consulting me first? Have you lost your fucking mind?" Brandon flung the paperwork from the bank at her, and it landed in the bathwater.

She shielded her face with her arm, fearing she was going

to be a blow to her head. She'd never seen Brandon so upset before. He was being so forceful that is was starting to turn her on. Mia knew she had to try to gain control of the situation. Her eye's softened and welled up with tears.

"I just picked up a couple of things for my mother. You know, you only got one, and I want to spoil her, every chance I get." Mia was hoping Brandon would understand because he'd often talked about how much he'd spoil his mother if she were still alive.

Mia definitely wouldn't spend that amount of money on that crackhead mother of hers, but someone had to account for all the goodies she'd bought for her significant other. Lately, Brandon would bitch about anything she bought herself, but that didn't stop her from doing it. He knew what type of woman she was when he'd married her. Just like he had a need for sex, she had a need for the finer things in life.

"Shouldn't your father be buying her expensive gifts? I mean, that is his wife."

"My father couldn't buy"—Mia almost forgot who she was talking to for a moment. Brandon still thought her parents were rich. She smiled lightly and tried again. "I meant, my father *could* buy her anything he wants, but should that stop me from treating her to a shopping spree? After all, it was her birthday."

Brandon's eyebrows wrinkled together, leaving a crease in the middle of his forehead. "All I'm trying to say is that you need to be a little bit more aware of where you spend *my* money."

"Your money?" Mia immersed herself deeper into the water. "You mean *our* money?"

"Whatever." Brandon walked out of the bathroom and slammed the door behind him.

He sat on the bed and rested his head in his hands. He

didn't even get into her buying that car. He was going to fix her. Tomorrow morning, he was going to take that car right back to the dealership. Her Benz was perfectly fine; she was just spending money to spend it.

*Mia just didn't get it*, Brandon thought. They were really on the brink of bankruptcy. He'd just bailed himself out by selling the label a few months back, and now he was in the same situation again.

Brandon had thought of a couple of people he could call to get some steady work but then decided against it. Going back to doing manual labor was out of the question. He didn't come this far to work a nine-to-five like regular people. By now, his money should have been long enough to sip cocktails on a private yacht overlooking the sunset in France. But his money-hungry wife was milking him dry. The only trip he could afford at this point was to the Jersey Shore.

Brandon was fed up with Mia's behavior. Her late nights out and drinking binges went from once a week to every other night. She would leave the house in the afternoon and wouldn't come home until three the next morning. Every time he asked where she'd been, she would claim that she was working. And the nanny, who was only supposed to work a few times a week, was taking care of their daughter more than she was.

Brandon lifted his head just as Mia exited the bathroom with a towel wrapped around her body. He looked over at Mia. He hadn't seen much of her lately, with her work schedule and all. He didn't even notice until now that she'd cut her hair, which now lay at the nape of her neck, and was neatly styled in an asymmetrical bob with whisky bangs. He always liked her better with short hair anyway, which complemented her bone structure perfectly. His eyes followed her around the room as she sat at her makeup table to do her daily makeup regimen.

Brandon stripped down to his boxer briefs and stood behind her, allowing his hard-on to touch the back of her neck.

Mia looked over her shoulder. "What do you think you're
doing?"

"Taking what's mine." Brandon gripped her up out of the
chair and pushed her toward the bed.

"Quit playing around. I told you I had a lunch date with
my mother," Mia said, trying to escape his tight hold.

Brandon grabbed her arm even tighter, leaving his hand-
print embedded in her skin. He yanked her out of the chair
and shoved her toward the bed. He threw her across the bed
and unwrapped her towel to reveal her tanned, naked body.

"Brandon, get off of me." Mia, struggling to get up off the
bed, hit him in the chest.

Brandon ignored her and continued to probe her body
with his husky hands. His mouth watered as he pried her legs
apart and looked at her neatly trimmed kitty. "I'm your husband, and I want some pussy. And you're going to give it to
me." He took his two fingers and rammed them up into her.
Then he pasted his body on top of hers, allowing her no room
to squirm around.

Brandon hadn't had sex in at least a month and was surely
due. He was sick and tired of playing games with Mia, who,
as a wife, was obligated to fuck him whenever he wanted, and
today he wasn't taking no for an answer.

Restraining her hands with his, Brandon parted her lips
and rammed her mouth with his tongue. He continued to
probe her body with his kisses, moving down to her chest. He
cupped her left breast in his hand and traced her nipple with
his tongue. He then pinched the nipples until they stood at
attention.

Mia struggled to push him off again, but as his mouth
left her chest and crept down to her belly button and in be-

tween her thighs, she decided to let him be. Her body shivered as Brandon parted the lips of her swollen pussy with his tongue and bit her clit in a playful manner. She ran her hands through his curly mane and grabbed his ears as he continued to taste her. It wasn't her intention to fuck Brandon, but it had been such a long time since he gave her some head, he was definitely going to get it.

Brandon grabbed her by the waist and pulled her closer to the foot of the bed, allowing her ass to rest on the wooden oak chest. He threw her long, slender legs over his muscular shoulders and nestled his face back into her sweet spot.

"Oh my God!" she said, breathing heavily

He looked up at Mia. "You like that, huh?"

"Baby, don't stop now," she said, pushing him back between her legs.

Brandon stuck his tongue deep inside her tight hole and hummed into her, causing her clitoris to vibrate wildly.

She arched her back in a spasm of uncontrollable pleasure. "Mmmmmm," she muttered, biting down on her bottom lip.

At that point, Brandon realized he had her right where he wanted her. He got up from off his knees and pulled his boxer briefs down to the floor. He stepped out of them and began stroking his hard-on.

Mia's pussy ached for mercy as Brandon prepared himself to enter her. He was taking long, and she was becoming more anxious by the second. "Give it to me, baby." She pulled his hips to her body and wrapped her legs around him.

"You want this dick?" Brandon pressed his hard-on against her pussy. "Huh?"

"Yeah, baby. Give me that big-ass dick." Mia grabbed his thick shaft and forced him up into her.

Brandon buried his throbbing dick deep inside her legs and began thrusting inside her sweetness. He panted heavily as he increased his speed, digging even deeper than before into her firm walls. He grasped her ass with the palms of his hands as they moved in unison to the same rhythm.

"Harder!" Mia shrieked. Sweat poured off her body, leaving an imprint on their silk sheets. She arched her back, thrusting her body forward to meet his.

Surprised at her demands, Brandon grabbed her by the waist and lunged into her tight walls with all his strength.

"Fuck me harder!" Mia demanded, digging her French-manicured nails into his back.

Brandon gyrated inside of her, letting out short, hard pumps. "Like that?"

"Oh yeah, baby," Mia purred, clawing at Brandon's breaking skin. "Like that. Yeah, baby, yeah, that's it. Fuck this pussy."

Brandon rolled over on his back and allowed Mia to climb on top of him. He grabbed her face in both hands and kissed her fervently as she bounced up and down on him, drenching his stiff hard-on with her juices. Brandon felt her walls retract as she came closer and closer to ecstasy.

"Oh, baby." Mia picked up her pace. "I'm gonna come all over this dick."

"That's right, baby, come all over this dick."

Mia threw her head back in satisfaction as the pleasure escaped her body in tingling waves. Brandon grabbed her hips and let out three long pumps, causing her to whimper as she continued to explode into pure bliss.

Mia rolled over onto her back, and Brandon mounted her, pushing his still rock-hard flesh into her mouth. He watched as her lips glided up and down on him as she fucked him with her mouth.

"That's right. Suck that dick." Brandon gently thrust his hips in the direction of her mouth.

Mia followed his orders and licked the length of his shaft like a cherry-flavored lollipop. She spat on it and accepted it back into her mouth.

Feeling himself about to release, Brandon backed off. "Open your mouth so you can taste daddy."

Mia opened her mouth wide, allowing come to splash down on her face. Brandon watched as she swallowed his come and opened her mouth, allowing him to see that it was gone. "That's my nasty girl." He kissed her on the mouth.

Mia smiled deviously and got up from the bed. She went into the bathroom and turned on the shower to get ready for her lunch date. Her aching pussy craved more than Brandon was able to give her. She locked the bathroom door and grabbed the dildo she had stashed behind the linens. She got into the tub and drew the curtain to the shower closed. She propped her right foot up on the faucet handles and inserted the 14-inch dildo inside her. She turned it up to the maximum speed and allowed it to consume her. She bit her lip as it swirled inside her with such force that it was making her knees weak. She held on to the tiled wall as she climaxed, moaning lightly only enough for her to hear.

Brandon lay back on the bed and folded his hands across his chest. He shook his head at the best sex he'd had yet with Mia. She'd tried to put up a fight, but with a little force, she was game.

He leaned over to the bedside table to check the time and noticed a missed call on his cell phone. He grabbed it off the table and flipped it open. There was a text message from Lynn canceling their lunch plans for today.

Brandon slammed the phone down. This was the second time this week she'd canceled on him. They'd been having lunch together faithfully for the last two months since he'd found out that she had a miscarriage, but this week, she seemed to be preoccupied with other people. Yesterday it was her cousin from out of town, the day before that it was a girl-friend from high school. Brandon knew she was lying.

Brandon heard the baby cry as soon as the phone hit the stand. He got up from the bed and put on the same boxer briefs he'd just pulled off. Leaving his cane to rest beside the bed, he walked across the hall and into the nursery. When he reached the crib, he leaned on it slightly and peeped over to see Kai wide-awake and staring into his eyes.

He picked her up from the crib and kissed her on the fore-head. He sat down in the rocker with her in his arms and patted her on the back. "I guess it's just me and you, sweetie," he whispered in her ear, as he continued to pat her lovingly on the back.

Brandon was upset about Lynn canceling their plans, but he'd rather spend the day with his daughter anyway. She loved him more than anyone did and to Brandon that was all he needed.

Mia covered her head with a cream-and-brown headscarf and tied it under her chin as she rode up to the parking level of the condo building. She paced back and forth in the eleva-tor, anxious to meet with the detective to see what new infor-mation he'd come up with.

The last time they met, he'd given her more than enough information about Lynn. So much information, she was able to meet Lynn at a support group for women who had miscar-riages.

With a little womanly charm, Mia and Lynn instantly clicked, and this was their second lunch date together this week. They'd spent many hours on the phone the last two weeks, talking about all sought of things, from movies to sex partners. Mia was really beginning to like Lynn. It was too bad that she was going to have to get hurt in the process of her making sure Brandon got what was coming to him.

Mia stepped off the elevator and placed her tortoise shell Gucci sunglasses over her eyes. Her tan trench coat flapped open at the bottom, revealing her long, slender legs as she trotted over to the black tinted-out Range Rover parked in the row designated for visitors.

She opened the door to the truck and slid in beside the detective. She opened her clutch, took out two stacks of cash totaling ten thousand dollars, and placed them on his lap. She then held her hand out and waited for him to turn over the information.

Detective Montgomery reached in the back seat and placed the manila envelope in her hand. Mia forced the envelope open, ripping it halfway across the top, and pulled out the papers. She shuffled through them, skimming each one individually.

She turned toward the detective. "So where's the bank account numbers for all of his other accounts? You know, the ones he was hiding from me?"

Detective Montgomery shook his head. "That's it, honey. There are no other accounts."

"There has to be."

"Hon, believe me, if he had another account, you would know about it. I'm afraid, there's nothing else on him, besides a few lunch dates with that Lynn girl."

"So what the fuck did I just pay you for?"

"I did do the job. It's not my fault the man didn't have anything to hide. If you ask me, he's just like all these other guys out here. He's a pretender. He made you think he was something he wasn't." Detective Montgomery gripped the steering wheel.

"I don't believe this shit." Mia looked down at the paper-work again. "This can't be happening. We're actually broke."

"You know, Mia, you did the same thing. You made him believe you were somebody you weren't."

"Fuck you!" Mia coolly placed her sunglasses back on her face. She opened the door to the car. "I will no longer need your services." She got out and slammed the door.

Detective Montgomery rolled down the window. "From the looks of things, you can't afford my services." He rolled the window back up and backed out of the parking space.

Walking over to her car, Mia noticed Brandon standing beside it with Kai in his arms. She placed the envelope Detective Montgomery gave her under her arm to shield it from his eyes and made her way over to him.

"Who was that?" Brandon asked, patting Kai on the back to comfort her.

"Just some man asking for directions." Mia pressed the unlock button on her keychain. "What are you doing up here anyway?" She opened the passenger side door to the car and placed her bag on the seat.

Brandon held out her monogrammed Louis Vuitton purse. "You forgot your wallet."

She grabbed the purse from his hand. "Thanks. I'll see you later." She pecked Brandon on the lips and walked around to the driver's side of the car. She backed out of the parking space and waved good-bye to him and the baby.

Mia looked at her watch. It was almost two p.m. She was supposed to meet her lunch date at two thirty, and the res-taurant was ten minutes away from the house on Second and South Streets.

Mia swerved in and out of traffic until she reached her loca-tion and parked the car with the valet. When she entered the restaurant, she noticed the table she reserved was still empty, meaning Lynn had yet to arrive. She stood behind an older white couple and waited to be seated.

Once at the table she ordered a glass of Chardonnay and sipped on it as she continued to wait for Lynn, who, by Mia's watch, was already ten minutes late. Just as Mia was about to open her menu, she noticed Lynn talking to the hostess, who led her to where Mia was sitting.

"Sorry I'm late." Lynn placed her Prada Nappa Hobo on the floor beside her chair.

Mia almost choked on her wine when that bag hit the floor. She didn't purchase it for Lynn to just fling down like an old napsack on trash day. She'd paid top dollar for that bag at Bergdorf Goodman and figured Lynn would treat it accordingly. She cleared her throat. "So, I see you're wearing the bag I bought you."

Lynn blushed. "Yes. Did I forget to mention how much I love it?"

"Well, if you love it so much, why are you dumping it on the floor like it's some sort of trash bag?"

"My bad." Lynn picked it up from the floor and placed it in the chair next to her. She took off her jacket and placed it in the same chair on top of her bag. Lynn didn't want Mia to think that she was being ungrateful. She loved the bag and the dress she'd bought her, which she was also wearing today. She took a seat across from Mia and picked up a menu to see what she wanted to order. She peeped over the menu at Mia, who was also looking at the menu and admired her.

"So, birthday girl, what's for lunch?" Mia opened up the menu in front of her.

"I don't know," Lynn replied, opening her menu to the appetizers. "I think I may start off with a tomato and basil soup."

Mia's face scrounged up. "You're going to eat soup on your birthday? You gotta be kidding me." She motioned for the waiter to come to the table.

"Yes, madam, what can I get for you?" he asked.

"Give me a bottle of your finest Chardonnay, and please make sure it's not that crap you served me earlier," she said in her most demanding voice. "I would also like to order two lobsters, and please make sure they're no smaller than three pounds."

Lynn watched in awe as the server tended to Mia's demands. She loved the way Mia commanded attention and had people eating out of her hands in a matter of seconds.

The table fell silent as they waited for the bottle of wine to arrive, both of them wondering what the other was thinking.

"So how was your business meeting this morning?" Lynn asked.

"It didn't go very well," Mia said, referring to her meeting with Detective Montgomery. "I wound up losing a lot of money in the investments I made."

"I'm sorry to hear that."

"So tell me about that mystery man of yours, what's his name Brandon?" Mia said changing the subject.

Lynn blushed like a little schoolgirl with a crush. "Well, we've been spending a lot of time together, you know, ever since I lost the baby and all. And, get this, the other night he told me he thinks he's falling in love with me."

Mia choked on her glass of wine to the point where the waiter had to come and pat her on the back. She didn't think the relationship between Brandon and Lynn had gotten that deep.

Once she stopped choking, she excused herself from the table and went into that bathroom to gather herself. "Okay, Mia," she said, looking at herself in the mirror, "go out there and play your part. She may have your man now, but not for long." She washed her hands at the sink and dried them off before re-applying her M•A•C Honeyflower lipstick. Then she exited the bathroom. *It's game time. I hope Lynn brought her gloves.*

Lynn waited patiently for Mia to return from the bathroom. She was wondering what she said wrong. All she could recall talking about was Brandon mentioning he loved her. *Maybe she is still upset because her husband left her.*

Mia had told Lynn that she was going through a violent divorce that almost left her out to dry. She'd mentioned the countless times he beat on her, telling her, it had gotten so bad, one night he tried to kill her and wound up dragging her down two flights of steps, causing her to lose her baby.

Lynn decided that she would no longer talk about Brandon to Mia and would try to support her newfound friend to the best of her ability. And if that meant keeping her mouth shut about how good things were going between her and Brandon, then that was the sacrifice she was willing to make.

# Chapter 6

### Dear Momma
### Chris

Chris patiently waited on the corner of 22$^{nd}$ and Jefferson, puffing on a Newport and watching his surroundings at the same time. It was early November, and the fall breeze kicked up heavily as the sun fell. He blew into his hands and rubbed them together to knock the chill off them. He looked down at his watch. It was now eight thirty p.m.

His young bull, De'Andre, the head of his street team, was late for their weekly meeting. This wasn't like his young bull at all. Chris suddenly got a bad feeling in the pit of his stomach that something had gone wrong. He looked down at his watch again.

Chris smoked the last of his cigarette, threw it to the ground, and stomped it out. He then dug into the right pocket of his hoodie and pulled out his cell phone. As he started dialing, he noticed his young bull walking up in a hurry. He flipped his phone shut and followed him over to the alleyway behind the poppy store. After trudging through a bunch of garbage and broken glass, he stopped under the only street lamp that lit the narrow pathway.

"Sorry, man." De'Andre dug into his Nike gym bag and pulled out a stack of cash. "I got caught over some bitch crib and lost track of time."

Chris snatched the stack from his hand. "Make sure that

shit don't happen again." He flipped through the cash and pulled out five hundred to pay his head worker. He held it out, and De'Andre gladly accepted it.

Chris looked over De'Andre's tall, slim build. His shoulders were so small, it looked as if the shirt he was wearing was still on the hanger. His short, nappy 'Fro peeped out of the sides of his fitted Phillies hat.

De'Andre began counting away his cut of the past week's profits. He noticed that Chris shorted him half of his money. "Damn, Chief! This was my first time being late. Cut me a break, man."

"What the fuck you mean, this was ya first time being late? Nigga, this a business. I need you to be on ya job. You think I care you was over some bitch house and you lost track of time? You better go as ask that bitch for the rest of your change 'cause, far as I'm concerned, nigga, you were on the clock." Chris placed the rest of the cash inside his hoodie, leaving a strange bulge in his clothing.

"That's some cold shit right there. You just gonna shit on me and not pay me all my dough? I'm out here grinding my ass off for you, making sure ya money right, and you gonna clip my cut 'cause I was a half hour late?"

Chris stepped further into the streetlight, which flickered down on his face. He took a deep breath in hopes of controlling his temper. "That's exactly why I'm clipping your cut. You my head nigga and you late. Business comes before anything, even your own family. If I can't trust you to be on time, then I can't trust you with my money."

"Yeah, a'ight."

De'Andre turned to walk out of the alleyway, but Chris grabbed him by the shoulder and spun him back around to face him. He looked into De'Andre's eyes, which were frozen with fear.

De'Andre reminded Chris of himself back in the day when he was just getting put on to the game. One of the old heads had done the same thing to Chris for being ten minutes late. He knew De'Andre was a loyal, trustworthy nigga, but he didn't need him getting sidetracked by a piece of ass.

"Look, just make sure you keep running a tight ship. If other niggas on deck see you slippin', they gonna try to take your place," Chris said, placing his hands in his pants pockets.

"Yeah, like Tank caught you slippin' huh?" De'Andre mumbled. He turned back around to exit out of the alley.

*Is this nigga really trying to come at me sideways?* Chris pulled his pistol out of the back of his pants and hustled behind De'Andre to catch up with him. Turning the gun around, he grasped it tightly by the barrel, allowing the butt of the gun to remain free. He grabbed De'Andre by the shoulder once more and came crashing down upon the side of his face with the butt of the gun.

"Agghh!" De'Andre yelped. He fell over two tin trashcans located at the end of the alley. "What the fuck is ya problem?"

Chris dragged him back into the darkness of the alleyway by his feet, under the dimly lit street lamp and placed his foot in the middle of De'Andre's chest. "You know what, Dre? Ya nut ass just got fired!" Chris barked. "I keep telling y'all niggas to stop testing me. You see what happened to Mike and Tank when they tried to run up on me. You don't want it wit' me young bull. Trust me, nigga!"

Chris grabbed the Nike duffel bag with the rest of the week's work from him and placed it on his own shoulder. He stood over De'Andre and shook his head as he watched him cradle the gash on the side of his head.

"Now you ain't gotta be late." Chris grinned, showing his chipped tooth.

"Fuck you, Chief!" De'Andre cradled his wounded head.

Chris kicked De'Andre in the side with his Timberland boot, causing him to bellow as he doubled over in pain. "No. Fuck *you!*"

Chris strolled out of the alleyway, making sure not to trip over the overturned trashcans, and headed over to his car, which was parked across the street from the poppy store. He got in and placed the Nike duffel bag beside him in the passenger seat. He then pulled out of the parking space with ease and honked the horn as he sped off down the street.

Chris felt bad for knocking De'Andre in the head with the gun, but he took it too far. *He should have just sucked that shit up and took the cut,* Chris thought. Chris had done it when he was a line soldier, and it made him wiser when it came to his money. He didn't care if he had to be late to his own momma's funeral, since business always came first.

Chris searched through the channels on the TV and came across the Thanksgiving Day Parade. Remembering watching it as a child with his mother and Brandon, it always served as the official start to the holiday season. He turned over to see if Shawn was awake, but he was still sound asleep.

Chris hadn't heard from his mother in a few weeks; he was so busy putting in work, by the time he got in the house at night, it was too late to call her. He planned to go over there today for Thanksgiving dinner anyway, so he decided to give her a call.

Chris waited for her to answer the phone, but after five rings, he knew she wasn't home because she answered the phone religiously on the second ring. *Where could she be?* Chris thought. It wasn't like her to be out on Thanksgiving morning. She usually spent the entire day in the kitchen.

Chris sat up on the side of the bed and rested his forearms

on his thighs. If it was any other day, he wouldn't be concerned, but something just wasn't right. He decided to call
Tracy's cell phone to see if she'd heard from her.

"Hello," Tracy said into the phone.

"What's up?" Chris got up from the bed and moved across
the room to the reclining chair. He didn't want to wake
Shawn, especially as he was talking to Tracy on the phone. He
wasn't in the mood for one of his tantrums.

"What you want?" Tracy whispered.

Chris could tell by the way she was talking that her nigga
must have been somewhere nearby. He wanted to ask her
what the hell her problem was, but he decided that was a
conversation for another day.

"You talk to Ma?"

"Nope. I called the house to wish her Happy Thanksgiving,
but she ain't answer."

"A'ight then. I'ma go past the house and see if everything is
cool. I'll get at you later."

Chris got up from the chair to grab a pair of pants and his
boots. He bent over and sifted through the pile of clothes
that lay at the bottom closet. Somehow, his and Shawn's
clothes got mixed up during laundry. Chris hated having another dude's underwear mixed in the bag with his own; it
just wasn't manly. He continued sifting through the bag of
laundry and came across a pair of gray polo sweatpants and a
thermal shirt to match. He grabbed his boots from the other
side of the room and sat down on the bed to put them on.

Shawn opened his eyes as Chris plopped down on the bed,
halfway sitting on his foot in the process. "Get off my foot."
He yawned.

"My fault," Chris said, slipping into his boot and lacing it
up.

Noticing Chris was in a hurry to get dressed, Shawn jumped

up from the bed and rambled in the closet to find something to wear. Chris wasn't going out of that door and leaving him all alone on a holiday to sit around his small-ass room.

Chris got up from the bed and searched the room for his car keys. He grabbed his State Property down coat from the chair, put it on, and turned to walk out the door. "I'll be back."

"Wait for me!" Shawn yelled, grabbing his navy blue pea coat from the closet.

"I said, I'll be back. Wait here."

Shawn sucked his teeth. "I always gotta wait here for you—I'm sick of this shit!"

"I'm going to check on my moms, and I'll be right back. Just chill, a'ight." Not giving Shawn the opportunity to respond, he locked the room door and headed down the steps and out of the building.

*That's it*, Shawn thought to himself, *I'm tired of this shit*. He slid his Louis Vuitton suitcase from under the bed and began packing his things. He was tired of playing second string to Chris's mother and that ugly baby momma of his. Chris was his man, and he should come before all of them.

Shawn finished throwing the last of his stuff into his matching overnight bag and placed it by the door. He then put on the stonewashed Rock and Republic jeans and the red long-sleeve Ben Sherman T-shirt he'd left on the bed. He laced up his Chucks, brushed his teeth, and headed out the door. No nigga was going to disrespect him; he didn't care how much money they had.

When Chris reached the car, he noticed a piece of looseleaf paper stuck to the windshield.

He snatched it off, leaving a mark on the windshield from

the gray electric tape that held it. He opened it up, and there in black letters cut out of newspaper he saw "Your Time Is Coming."

Chris crumpled the note up and tossed it in the middle of the street. This wasn't the first time someone had threatened his life. If he got paranoid over each little incident, he would never make any money.

He got in the car and sped off heading toward his mother's house. He drove up Diamond Street and made a left on Broad Street. He followed Broad Street all the way up until he reached the Roosevelt Boulevard, and made another left, heading out to Northeast Philly. He reached his mother's house in a record-breaking fifteen minutes. He drove up into the driveway and turned the car off.

Ms. Ethel, the next-door neighbor, was standing on the porch, peeking into the living room window. Chris walked up the steps and stood silently behind her, startling her. "How you doin', Ms. Ethel?"

"Chris, honey, how are you?" She kept peering into the window.

"Have you talked to my mother?" Chris was now fascinated himself with looking inside the house.

"I spoke with her last night before she went to bed. She said she would be up bright and early to put her bird in the oven."

"Yeah. I called her this morning, and she didn't answer."

"Do you have a key?" Ms. Ethel tried to lift the window open with her fragile arms, but it was locked.

"Naw, but I know how to get in."

Chris walked around the side of the house to the kitchen window. He forced it open and hoisted himself inside as he had done plenty of times when he'd misplaced his keys. After tumbling onto the kitchen floor, he went over to the front door and unlocked it for Ms. Ethel, who headed straight up the steps, as he continued to search the first floor of the house.

Chris looked around the living room and saw everything neatly arranged, right down to the three throw pillows on the sofa. He went to grab the Bible that lay open on the coffee table as if she was in the midst of morning prayer.

Ms. Ethel screamed from the top of the steps, "Oh Jesus! Chris, come quick!"

Chris jolted up the steps and saw his mother in the middle of the bathroom floor, a bottle of medication in her hand. He grabbed the case of pills and read the label—Vasotec. *Take twice daily with a meal.* "What is this medicine she has in her hands?"

Ms Ethel examined the bottle at the same time. "That's that heart medication they put her on after she had the stroke."

"Stroke? What stroke?" Chris placed the bottle on the sink and kneeled down next to his mother.

"Your mother had a mild stroke four months ago. She didn't tell you because she didn't want to worry you. She was more concerned about getting you and Brandon back together. Remember when she said she was going out of town to visit your great aunt in Virginia? Well, she was in the hospital the entire time."

"I can't believe this is happening." He grabbed her wrist to check her pulse. "She's still alive! Call an ambulance!" He wiped the tears away from his eyes.

Ms. Ethel scrambled down to his mother's room and dialed 9-1-1.

Chris really felt bad that his mother thought she had to lie to him about her whereabouts because of his feud with Brandon. Having a stroke was a serious deal. Even he knew that.

"Mom! Mom! Can you hear me?"

Her body remained limp as he continued to talk to her. She could hear him, but she was unable to answer.

Chris heard his own heart beating fast. He took some deep breaths and tried to focus on his mother. "Hold on, mom. The ambulance is coming." He pulled her into his arms and brushed her salt-and-pepper hair out of her face. He kissed her on the forehead.

Chris could hear the sirens at the top of the block. "I love you, Mom," he repeated several times before the rescue team arrived.

The EMTs rushed into the bathroom and moved her into the hallway so she could be placed on the gurney. Chris stood aside as they lifted her up and strapped her down. They carefully took her down to the steps and placed her in the back of the rescue wagon.

Ms. Ethel climbed into the back of the ambulance. "Are you coming?"

"I'ma lock up, and I'll be right there."

Chris snatched his mom's Bible from the coffee table and hurried out the door. He got in the car and placed the Bible in the back seat. He backed out of the driveway and drove over to the Northeast Medical Center.

When he arrived at the medical center, Ms. Ethel was standing by the entrance to meet him. "Is she okay?"

"I'm afraid not. The doctors say her heart is failing. She's going in to have surgery in the morning."

Chris backed away from Ms. Ethel and left back out of the hospital doors. He wasn't ready to accept the fact that his mother may not live past tomorrow. He ran back to the car and grabbed her Bible from the back seat.

He jogged back into the hospital and followed Ms. Ethel to his mother's room. He walked in the door, and there sat Brandon by the bed holding Ms. Ruth's hand. "Who the hell called this clown?"

"Fuck you!" Brandon jumped to his feet, leaving his cane resting on the floor.

Ms. Ethel stood stunned in the middle of the doorway. She would have never called Brandon if she knew it was going to cause this type of riff. Ruth had begged her to do so on their way to the hospital, and Ms. Ethel just couldn't tell her no. She was familiar with the situation between the two, and had warned Ruth that it may be a big mistake having both of them in the room together, but Ruth wouldn't have it any other way.

Without warning, Chris pulled his pistol from the back of his pants and aimed it at Brandon. "No! Fuck you, nigga! You gonna send my own homie to kill me and you really think I'm going to let you leave this hospital room alive? You must be out of your mind."

Ignoring the pain in his right side, Brandon continued toward Chris. He pulled a nickel-plated .45 from the inside pocket of his Burberry toggle coat and pointed it at Chris as well. "Are you really ready to play this game?"

"I want my money." Chris moved closer in Brandon's direction. "You know I don't have a problem laying you down. Look at how easy I got in ya crib. Nigga, you ain't nothing to me."

"What money? Nigga, please. You cashed that in when you raped my wife. I don't owe you shit. The only thing you gonna get from me is this bullet to ya skull."

"Ya wife?" Chris sucked his teeth. "Man, that chick a stone-cold ho. I fucked that bitch before you even met her. Go ahead . . . ask her about the deal she made me."

"Bullshit. She wouldn't fuck you. You ain't even her type." Brandon chuckled at the thought of Chris even getting close to a woman of Mia's stature.

"Nigga, the only reason you're her type is because she thought you had some money. If you would have did a little asking around, you would have found out that she was trash, just like all the other hoes you fuck with. She's a pretender. That bitch ain't got no real money; she after yours. You out here claiming a fuck gone wrong."

"You stinkin' muthafucka," Brandon said, moving around the hospital bed to zero in on Chris.

Chris squinted his left eye in hopes of getting an exact shot to Brandon's chest. In the heat of the moment, he had forgotten what he was doing there. His hatred for Brandon beat loudly in his chest; his face turned bright red as he bit his lip and leaned in on the trigger. *Squeeze it just a little harder,* he told himself. *That nigga is in the way. He gotta get laid down.*

Ms. Ethel jumped in front of Chris.

"Stop it! You hear me! Stop it right now!" Ms. Ruth said, straining in between words.

All the commotion had awakened her from her rest. She opened her weary eyes and looked at the two men standing over her with guns drawn at each other. With Brandon on her right side and Chris on her left, she didn't know who to reason with. Both of them wore the look of hate and betrayal on their faces.

"What is wrong with you two?" she whispered, looking back and forth at the both of them. "I didn't raise you to be like this." Tears started splashing down her face. "I told Ethel to call Brandon. I wanted him here."

Chris loosened his grip on the trigger and slowly lowered his gun, his face still twisted up in disgust. Brandon wasn't her real son, he was.

As "I wanted him here" rolled off his mom's tongue, Chris realized his hatred for Brandon went way past the money he took from him. Growing up, Brandon easily became his mother's favorite. He remembered having to give up his room for the smaller one down the hall when Brandon came to live with them. She treated him with so much love and affection, always praising him for jobs well done and good grades, but had never said thanks once to Chris for putting food on the table. Chris had always craved attention from his mother and figured, as long as he provided her with money, she would show him the same attention she showed Brandon. It never happened that way, and till this day, he was still trying to gain the love and affection he felt he deserved.

"I'm out of here," Chris said, walking toward the door.

"Chris," Ms. Ruth said sternly, "sit down."

Chris stood in the doorway of the hospital room. He placed his hands in his pockets and looked down at his shoes and sucked his teeth. *Who the hell does she think she's talking to? I'm a grown man.*

"You two should be ashamed of yourselves," she said, eyeing both of them. "I raised you as brothers. And even if you can't settle your differences, you can at least be civil to each other."

Chris looked over at Brandon and he too now wore a look of shame on his face. She was right; they were brothers. Brandon let that wannabe high-class ho, Mia, cloud his mind. She had broken them apart. Before she came along, they were hanging out, getting money, and living the high life. Their business was doing well, and they were on their way to the top of the music world.

Chris knew he should have stuck to his gut instinct and told her to fuck off when she approached him about hooking her up with him, but when she offered him a piece of that fine yellow ass, he just couldn't resist. She sucked Chris's dick so good that he was ready to wife her himself. She was indeed good at what she did, manipulating niggas and making herself look like the victim all at the same time. Chris was hip to her shit and knew it wasn't going to be long before Brandon found himself in a financial bind.

When Chris finally hooked them up, he noticed a change in Brandon's attitude. His confidence turned to arrogance. He tried to overlook it, but when Brandon stole money from the safe, to keep up his expensive lifestyle, he wound up punching him in the jaw. He knew Brandon didn't use that money to pay for the New Year's party for the record label. He'd checked with the event coordinators and found out it was all paid for by the advertisers. That was the first time they had ever gotten physical with each other, all because of money and a bitch.

While Chris felt like rape was a harsh word, he did have sex with her without her full permission. But he justified his actions on the fact that he had fucked her before.

At first, she was into it, moaning and groaning as he tasted her sweet pussy, but when she turned the light on and found out it was Chris, not Brandon, she went bananas. He didn't understand why. If his memory served him right, his dick was way bigger than Brandon's anyway.

Mia liked rough sex, so he figured her saying no meant yes. He recalled the one time they fucked and she told him not to put it in her ass, but he did it anyway, and she enjoyed every minute of it.


"Listen, you two," Ms. Ruth started. "I want this ended right now. I can't go to my Maker knowing the two people I love more than anything in the world are still fighting."

"Aww, Ma. Don't talk like that." Chris left the door and took a seat on the bed beside her. He grabbed her hand and placed it in his. "You ain't going nowhere. You gonna be fine." He looked over at Brandon, who still had the gun aimed at his head.

Ms. Ruth looked at Brandon. "Put that gun down, son. I didn't bring you here for that."

Brandon's hand shook as he lowered the gun and placed it back into his coat. He stood at the foot of the bed with his arms folded, still gritting on Chris.

Chris ignored Brandon's advances and focused on his mother. For the first time in his life, he was now the good son.

"Promise me," Ms. Ruth's voice squeaked. "Promise me that you two will end this nonsense."

Chris glanced over at Brandon and then at his mother. Feuding with him was starting to take too much energy away from what really had to be done, which was making money. Brandon was going to get his sooner rather than later with that scandalous ho of his. She was sure to make his life miserable. "I don't know, Ma."

"Yeah, I second that. He has to pay for all the grief he's caused me and my family."

"Now wait a minute," Ms Ruth said, raising her fragile voice. "You haven't been no angel yourself. Both of you are at fault. I'm not asking you to kiss and make up. I'm asking you to be civil." She repeated for the second time.

Chris squeezed his mother's hand tighter. If she was going through all of this trouble to get them to stop warring against each other then he would at least try. If Brandon even thought about flinching the wrong way, he was going to rock him.

"You know what, Ma? If it's going to make you happy, you got it." Chris leaned in and kissed her on the forehead.

"Whatever." Brandon grabbed his cane from the floor and moved toward the door. "I'll be outside in the waiting room if you need me." He left out of the room and proceeded to the waiting area.

Chris ignored Brandon's nonchalant attitude and went

back to concentrating on his mother. He wasn't worried at all and knew she would be okay. She was a strong woman, and he had faith that she would be around for years to come.

Chris rubbed his mother's hand as she drifted in and out of sleep, and he wound up nodding off himself.

When he awoke, it was three in the afternoon. He knew Shawn was going to have a fit about him being out that long, but his mother came first. No matter how many times Chris told him, he still didn't get the picture.

He carefully placed his mother's hand by her side and kissed her on the cheek. He got up from the chair and crept out the door.

Ms. Ethel got up from her chair and followed him out the door. She pulled the door, so she wouldn't wake Ms. Ruth. "Chris, honey, where are you going?"

"I gotta go take care of some business. I'll be back tonight."

"Sweetheart, make sure you come back, you hear? Your mother needs you." Ms. Ethel buttoned her sweater to ward off some of the breeze in the hallway.

"I know," Chris said, walking down the hall. "I know."

Chris walked swiftly down the corridor and to the elevators. He noticed Brandon was still sitting in the waiting room with, his mouth wide open, snoring like a hog. He shook his head as he pressed the button for the main floor. He got into his car and made his way back to his crib.

When he arrived, he was relieved that Shawn wasn't there. He sat down on the bed and flipped on the TV. He didn't feel like dealing with his bullshit anyway. He did, however, feel like seeing his son. Plus, he needed to tell Tracy about Ma.

He dialed her number and waited for her to answer.

"Hello?" A deep mellow-toned voice answered.

"Who's this?" Chris looked at his phone to see if he'd dialed the right number.

"Nigga, didn't I tell you to stop calling my wife?"

It was Hakeem, Tracy's so-called husband.

Chris gritted his teeth. "Fuck you! I want to see my son. Now put Tracy on the phone."

"She busy right now, sucking my dick," Hakeem chuckled. "Don't call this phone no more, homie. I ain't gonna tell you again."

"Fuck you, pussy! I'ma see you. I'm definitely gonna holla at you about something."

"Oh yeah? Well, I'm pretty sure you know where to find me."

Chris could hear his son crying in the background. He clenched his fist in anger. "Is that my son crying like that? You better not put your hands on him."

"Nigga, that's *my* son, and don't worry about what's going on in *my* house."

Chris's blood was boiling. He wanted to tell Tracy that Ma was sick, and this stupid nigga was playing games. He noticed his cell phone was ringing; it was Tracy's number again.

"Nigga, what the fuck do you want?" Chris said answering the phone.

"Chris, it's me," Tracy whispered into the phone. "I need your help. Please."

Chris could hear the urgency in her voice. "You know where to meet me."

"I won't be able to meet you until he goes to sleep. I'll text you when I'm on my way."


Tracy hung up the phone and placed it back on the coffee table just as Hakeem had left it. If he knew she called Chris back, he would kill her.

Last night, he came in drunk and demanded sex while in front of Li'l Chris. When she refused him, he yelled and screamed at the top of his lungs and slapped her in the face right in front of her son.

She looked at Li'l Chris, who sat quietly in the corner of the living room playing with his fire engine truck. She had to get him out of here. It was no telling what Hakeem was capable of.

She planned it out in her mind. Hakeem slept like a log. She would go to bed like she normally did, and when he was sound asleep, she would gather as many belongings as she could, and her and Li'l Chris would be gone.

Tracy bathed Li'l Chris and got him ready for bed around nine thirty. She hid two small duffel bags in the linen closet located in the bathroom. Her keys and purse were both stashed under the sink amongst the cleaning supplies. She usually had Li'l Chris in bed and 'sleep by this time every night, but she was trying to kill time. That way, when she went to bed, Hakeem would most likely be 'sleep already.

She tucked Li'l Chris in and kissed him on his forehead. She rubbed her hand through his sandy red hair. Even at the early age of two, he was the spitting image of his father. She turned off the lights to his Buzz Lightyear-inspired room and traveled down the hall to her room.

Hakeem was already dozing off, just like she suspected, when she got in the bed. She turned her back to him and faced the wall. To Tracy, it seemed as though it took hours for Hakeem to fall asleep.

As soon as she heard the first snore, she was out of there, slipping out of bed and into the bathroom, where she had a bag of clothes in the linen closet. She closed the bathroom door, locked it, and proceeded to get dressed. Just as she fastened her jeans, she heard a soft knock at the door.

"Babe, I'm sorry. I just got carried away. I promise it won't happen again. Let's go to bed," Hakeem whispered, turning the knob on the door.

Tracy looked in the bathroom mirror at her eye, which was starting to swell. "You promise?" she said, tears forming in the corner of her eyes.

"Yeah, I said I promise. Baby, I love you." He leaned his forehead against the door.

Tracy unfastened her jeans and slipped them off just as easily as she had put them on. "I love you too."


Chris grabbed his hammer from the television stand and rushed out the door. When he reached his car, all four tires were flat. He started banging on the hood of the car.

He immediately began searching for another mode of transportation, walking up and down several blocks around his home, searching for an older-model car to hot-wire. He came across a tan Delta 88 and looked around to see if anyone was looking.

Once the coast was clear, Chris smashed the window open and hopped in. He quickly opened the control panel under the dash and started the car. He swerved off in a hurry toward his and Tracy's agreed destination.

Chris finally got to the meeting spot over an hour late. He stood in the middle of the dirt parking lot by the old horse stables where they always met and was surprised that Tracy wasn't there. He sat in his car for about an hour waiting for her to come.

Every time he called her cell phone, it went straight to voicemail. He hoped like hell that Hakeem didn't do anything crazy. He was on Chris's shit list as is, and the only reason Chris hadn't handled him yet was because Tracy had begged him not to, telling him she had everything under control.

After waiting around in the dark parking lot for Tracy for two hours, Chris knew that she had most likely changed her mind. This wasn't the first time she'd called him to rescue her from Hakeem; it was actually becoming more of a bi-weekly thing. And Chris went every time she called. He turned on the lights to the car and made his way back to his boarding house.

# Chapter 7

## Sheisty
## Brandon

Brandon found himself in a slump ever since he'd found out about Ms. Ruth's illness. He felt like he was losing his mother all over again. He didn't sleep much and spent more time at home with his family than being out and about in the streets. Well, he spent more time with Kai. Mia was too busy doing her. She was still staying out late and spending money like it was going out of style.

Brandon was now down to a measly fifty thousand dollars in the bank. Things were so tight, he demanded Mia return the Maserati she'd leased several months ago. What bothered him the most about his wife was, before they married, she was at least willing to try to cook, clean, and tend to his manly needs. But now, she could care less if he had anything to eat. And she hired a housekeeper to keep their condo in order in her absence.

Brandon was getting an itch for some pussy. They hadn't had sex since early October, and it was damn near Christmas. Any other time, he would have called one of his old hoes, and they would have been thrilled to give him a piece of ass. He was trying his best to be a good husband and an even better father, and the only thing standing in his way was his relationship with Lynn. He hadn't had sex with her in quite some time, but there wasn't a minute that passed that it didn't cross his mind.

Mia was becoming more of a hassle than Brandon antici-
pated. She'd turned into a completely different person over
the last few months, and he had no idea who she was anymore. He hated to admit it, but the painful things Chris had
said about his wife while they were at the hospital were turning out to be true.

There was no doubt about her being money-hungry, and
after finding a few condoms in her purse, she was checking
out to be a whore also. When Brandon confronted her about
them, she told him that she'd bought them for him and her
to use during sex because she didn't want to take birth control
pills. Brandon had never stooped that low as to search her
things, but her whereabouts just wasn't adding up.

He spoke to her agent, Gregory, two weeks ago and learned
that Mia never went back to work. In fact, she'd turned down
every job he offered her, telling him she was retiring from
the modeling business to become a stay-at-home mom. When
Brandon confronted her about that, she claimed she'd found
a new agent and didn't want to hurt Gregory's feelings.

Mia had an answer for everything, so Brandon was in search
of more concrete information to use in his defense because,
at this point, he was looking more like an insecure husband
than a confident mate.

It was one p.m. on New Year's Day, and Mia had yet to get
home from the previous night. He called her cell phone several times, only for it to go voicemail. Pacing around the living
room with Kai in his arms, Brandon's mind wandered in the
worst way. *What if she's dead, or in a bad car accident?*

He decided to try her cell phone again. He headed into the
bedroom and grabbed the cell phone from the bed. He tried
her cell phone once again, and this time it started ringing.
He waited patiently for her to answer, but she never did. He
threw the phone on the couch and went back to the bedroom.

Brandon laid Kai on her back in the middle of their bed and went over to Mia's closet. He opened it up and took a long look at the countless designer outfits neatly aligned with the price tags still attached. He was glad that he decided to skip buying Christmas gifts this year, because Mia didn't need another Jimmy Choo or Prada pump to add to her overflowing collection.

He started taking them off the hangers and placing them in a pile beside the bed. They were his clothes anyway; his money had bought them, and if she couldn't bring her ass home, then she didn't deserve to own such expensive garments. Brandon knew that he most likely would be unable to take them back to the store, and he knew no one other than Mia who wore a size two, tall.

As he was taking the clothes down off the racks, a small box fell from the closet and spilled over onto the floor. Brandon stopped in his tracks, threw the paisley pink Prada blouse he had in his hand in the pile with the rest of the clothes, and bent down to gather the spilled items from the box. He noticed several bank and credit card statements under the name Latifah inside. Brandon looked at the mailing address on the Saks credit invoice, a P.O. Box. This was undeniably strange. Brandon didn't recall Mia mentioning anyone named Latifah. With a name like that, he wasn't sure if he wanted to know who the hell Latifah was. He put the statements back in the box and placed it back neatly on the top shelf of her closet.

Brandon took a seat on the bed where Kai was lying. He smiled and kissed her on the forehead as she cooed at him. He grabbed her up in his arms and rocked her back and forth. Having Kai was the best thing Mia had ever done in her life, in Brandon's eyes. Other than that, she was worthless.

Kai's little hands clawed at his face. He accepted them into his mouth and nibbled on them, causing her to laugh. He held her out in front of him and looked at her pretty smile. Kai had changed Brandon's life in ways that he didn't think could ever happen.

Brandon took being a parent seriously. He took her to every doctor's visit, and even attended parenting classes. He didn't care if he was stuck in the house with her day after day, she was his daughter, and she needed him more than anybody.

He looked at her little brown face and fell in love with her all over again. Her jet-black curly mane was now almost four inches long. He stared into her eyes. She was the spitting image of her mother. Kai made him want to be a better man.

Brandon missed his mother now more than ever. He only wished his mother could be here to see her. She would be so proud that her son had such a beautiful little girl. Mia's mother never came and visited Kai. She always sent her well-wishes through Mia. Brandon knew that if his mother was alive, she would have camped out in Kai's room. Brandon was the only family Kai had on his side of the family, and he intended on being there for her forever and a day.

He tried Mia's phone one last time. Just as the answering machine picked up, he heard the lock on the front door click as if someone had slid a key card through it.

Brandon hurried across the hall to the nursery and placed Kai in her crib for her afternoon nap. As he closed the door behind him, he noticed Mia sitting on the oak chest at the foot of the bed, taking her heels off. She looked up at him and quickly looked away.

*How could she just waltz up in here after being out all night and not at least explain her actions?* Brandon stormed across the hall and gripped her up, breaking the spaghetti strap to her Roberto Cavalli gown.

"What the hell are you doing?" she asked, clawing at his face in attempt to break free from his grasp.

"I'm sick of this shit. Where the hell were you?" He threw her onto the bed and ripped her dress off.

She tried to push him off. "Have you lost your mind?"

"I asked you a question!" he said pinning her down in between his muscular thighs.

"I was—"

"Answer me!"

Mia looked into Brandon's face and took a deep breath. She knew her staying out late had to come to an end. She was only doing it to get back at him anyway. It wasn't necessary at this point in her planning for his demise, but she thought it was fun all the same.

Before she could say anything, his hot hand smacked her face in a rampage. Her body tensed up in shock as he shook her body uncontrollably.

"Stop! You're hurting me!"

Brandon stopped in his tracks and backed off of her. *What am I doing? I never hit a woman in my life.* He walked out of the bedroom and into the living room in a trance. He grabbed his jacket from the coat rack and walked out of the door without a thought to where he was going.

Mia got up from the bed and noticed her closet was completely cleaned out, and all her expensive gowns and garments splattered across the oak floor.

She dug into one of the trash bags and saw her ivory Fendi cashmere sweater dress inside. *Oh my God!* She ran over to the closet to check and see if her important papers were still there. She hoped like hell he didn't come across them.

She reached up to the top shelf and returned with the gray tin box that held her past life inside. She opened up and eyed through the paperwork; everything seemed to be in perfect order. She still wanted to be cautious as to what she left in their home. If he rummaged through her closet once, there was no doubt in her mind he would do it again.

Mia left the tin box on the bed, hurried to the living room closet, and returned with a paper shredder and shredded the documents into a million pieces. She then dumped her clothes out of the trash bags and used one of them to bag up the shredded documents. She ran down the hall to the incinerator and dumped it in.

After returning from the incinerator, Mia noticed that her face was beginning to feel awfully hot. She went back into the bedroom to look into the dresser mirror. The right side of her face was red as a beet, and becoming more swollen by the minute. She sucked her teeth and continued to stare at the welt across her face.

Brandon had gone too far. Yes, she was wrong for not coming home last night, but how dare he put his hands on her?

Mia left out of the bedroom and sauntered into the kitchen to grab a bad of frozen mixed vegetables from the freezer. She held it on her face in hopes of reducing the swelling.

It was no way he was going to get away with putting his hands on her. She knew exactly where he would end up tonight, so it was time to throw a little salt in his game. She called Lynn up and invited her to a late coffee date at this little shop on 19th and Chestnut.

Several hours and eleven glasses of Seagram's Gin on the rocks later, Brandon found himself standing in front of Lynn's apartment building. He disregarded the front desk attendant and headed straight for the elevators.

He brushed himself off and checked his breath as his rode up to the ninth floor. He pulled his emergency Issey Miyake cologne from his inside jacket pocket and sprayed it on his neck and clothes. He didn't call ahead, but he hoped like hell Lynn was home. He needed her company tonight and had no other place to turn.

He stepped off the elevator and stumbled down the hall until he reached her apartment. He banged on the door and waited for a response.

As soon as Lynn opened the door, Brandon pressed his lips against hers and pushed his way inside the apartment. Using his foot to close the door behind him, he continued to explore Lynn's mouth with his tongue.

Lynn closed her eyes as she accepted Brandon's hot, lingering tongue between her parted lips. Her mind was telling her to push him away because he was indeed a married man, but her body was telling her to let him have his way. She loved this man, and even though she would most likely never be the woman he would be with, she wanted to at least enjoy the moment. She kept moving back into the apartment, until she found herself being pushed over the arm of the couch, Brandon's heavy body covering her as he continued feeding from the wetness of her mouth.

He pulled away from her to stare into her light brown eyes. "You know it was a year ago today when we met?"

Lynn was surprised that he remembered, and began to reminisce.

She was a bartender at a small pub in Center City. It was New Year's Day, and Brandon stormed into the bar and demanded a glass of Seagram's Gin on the rocks. Busy washing out glasses, Lynn took her time getting to him, and Brandon became annoyed. When she turned around to see who was making such a fuss, she was blown away. Brandon's tall black muscular frame made her pussy wet just as it did every time she saw him after that.

A simple fuck would have been okay with Lynn, but Brandon seemed to want more. Lynn had no plans on falling for

him, but she just couldn't help it. He was a perfect gentle-
man, and he was the only man who really took interest in her
schooling.

That's the reason why she was so shaken up when she
found out that he was married, that his name wasn't Keith
but Brandon. That was the day when he broke her heart, and
she hadn't been the same since.


"Damn, I love you," Brandon said, whispering in between
smooches.

Stunned by his words, Lynn opened her eyes and snapped
out of her daze. She pushed him off and gazed into his chocolate brown face. She palmed his face and rubbed his stubble.
"What did you say?" She looked up at him as if she might have
heard him wrong. She could smell the liquor on his breath.

Brandon kissed her once more tenderly on the lips and
then with a straight face said, "I said I love you."

Brandon was drunk and a little out of sorts, but he did love
Lynn. He always felt strongly about her, but money, which
she had almost none of, always brought him back to reality.
She was a beautiful, intelligent young woman who could, if
given the right tools, take the world by storm.

Brandon pushed her sandy brown Afro out of her face,
revealing her most mesmerizing features. When they'd first
met, her Afro was a bright golden red. Her soft honey brown
skin held no abrasions.

Her long captivating eyelashes and full, pouted lips aroused
Brandon. He circled her lips with his index finger, imagining
it was his dick, and she accepted it into her mouth. Brandon
continued to probe her curvaceous body with his hands, and
felt himself rise to full erection.

Brandon had come to realize that Lynn was more of a wom-

an than Mia could ever be, that she was the one he was supposed to marry. He wished that Lynn was Kai's mother, and
never got over her losing the baby she was carrying for him.

In fact, he'd spent the last few months thinking of what
life would be like, raising a child and having a family with
Lynn. Yes, she was younger than Mia, but for a young girl,
she had a good head on her shoulders. Lynn was graduating
from college in the spring and had already secured a position
as a journalist at the *Philadelphia Tribune*. Although journalists
don't make much money, Brandon respected for her doing
something she loved.

"But your wife?" Lynn rubbed her hand through his curly
mane.

That was the last person Brandon wanted to think about
right now.

He lifted Lynn's navy blue Gap T-shirt over her head,
revealing her black, laced bra. He threw the T-shirt to the
ground and went to work on the bra. With his thumbs, he
slid the straps of her bra off her shoulders. Brandon palmed
her swollen, D cup-size breasts with his extra-large hands and
nestled his face in between them.

As Lynn's smoother-than-silk skin rubbed against his
sprouting beard, he felt like a little kid being buried in his
mother's bosom, safe, secure, and at ease. Lynn continued to
rub her hands through his hair, and Brandon cuddled even
closer to her bosom with each stroke.

He captured her left nipple between his lips and nibbled
away at it, and Lynn threw her head back and bit her bottom
lip as he left a wet trail from her nipples down to her belly
button with his tongue.

Brandon unfastened her jeans and inched them down to
her ankles and then off to the floor. He grabbed Lynn's perfectly polished foot and placed her toe in his mouth, massaging it.

Lynn breathed heavily as he left one foot and moved on to the other. She grabbed at his shirt, popping the buttons off as she ripped it open and revealed his muscular chest. "I want you now," she whimpered, grabbing at his Versace belt buckle.

Lynn could hear the phone ringing from the bedroom. When she looked at the clock, she noticed it was eight p.m. She'd promised her friend Nina that she would meet her at the coffee shop a half-hour ago, but that was before Brandon arrived.

"Wait a minute." She jumped up from the couch and dashed into the bedroom to grab the phone. "I was supposed to have coffee with a friend, and I just know that was her calling on the phone. I have to call her back and let her know that I'm not coming."

Lynn dialed the number and sat back down next to Brandon, who had already loosened his pants. He was a little annoyed that she got up in the middle of their session to make a phone call, but he wasn't going to allow that ruin the mood.

"Where are you?" Mia asked. "You were supposed to be here a half and hour ago."

"I got caught up at home. I won't be able to make it." Lynn swatted at Brandon, who was nibbling on her ear.

"Are you fucking serious? You could have called me a little earlier, you know," Mia yelled, causing the entire coffee shop to look at her. She rolled her eyes at the patrons. "What the hell are you staring at?"

Brandon became startled when he heard what sounded like Mia's voice through the phone. He knew it anywhere; there weren't too many females who could pull off the phone sex voice like Mia could. *It couldn't be.* He stopped nibbling on Lynn's ear and pushed the phone away from her mouth before she could answer. "What's your friend name?" he asked casually.

"Why do you want to know?" Lynn shot back playfully.

Brandon gave her a serious look, and she wiped the smile right off her face.

"Her name is Nina. I met her at a support group for women who have lost children."

*That couldn't be Mia*, Brandon thought, relieved. She hadn't lost a child. But that was damn sure a strong coincidence.

Mia screamed through the phone line. "Did you just put me on hold?"

"Well, tell Nina you have to call her back. Daddy's home, and he wants to play." Brandon began nibbling at her ear again.

"Stop it," Lynn said, trying not to giggle into the phone.

Mia could hear Brandon in the background. Her pressure shot up so fast, her entire body was covered in sweat. She knew he was going to end up over there, but hearing his voice on the other end of the phone, at another woman's house, angered her even more. She wanted to waltz up into that apartment building and blow his head off.

Mia hung up the phone on Lynn. She sat at the table alone sipping on a mocha latte. Getting Lynn to do what she wanted was going to be harder than she thought. She looked at her cell phone, and out of nowhere, threw it across the coffee shop, just missing one of the employees in the head as it smashed into the wall. She grabbed her purse and her fur jacket and left out in a huff.

The phone went dead, and Lynn turned the cordless off and threw it over the side of the couch.

"Can we get back to business now?" Brandon unzipped his pants and stepped out of them.

He stood in front of Lynn as she sat on the edge of the couch. She looked up at his broad muscled chest. His chocolate skin curved so graciously through the tightness of his stomach. While Brandon wasn't as in-shape as he used to be, he still had the body of a God. His rippled arms flexed as placed them on his lean hips.

Lynn tugged at his Armani boxer briefs. "We sure can." She pulled his briefs down past his thighs, licking her lips at the sight of his swollen flesh. She became wet between the thighs as she grasped it with both hands and began stroking him off.

Brandon didn't even want her to suck him off. He would rather feel her walls close in on him. He grabbed her up off the couch and led her to the bedroom. He and Lynn was having too many quickies. He wanted to show her how much he really cared for her, and that he couldn't do from the couch.

He pushed Lynn down on the bed and ripped off her bikini cut underwear. He pulled her naked body close to his and held her tight.

Lynn listened to his heartbeat, as she did every time she was in his arms. His manly body engulfed her like the womb of an unborn child. She pulled away from him and looked up at him. "Do you really love me?"

He kissed her sweetly on the lips as he did earlier. "Yes."

Lynn backed away from him and lay across the bed, her thick thighs wide open, revealing the lusciousness of her neatly trimmed kitty and her hooped clit ring.

Brandon hovered over her and continued caressing her stomach and playing with her belly ring. He grabbed Lynn's wide hips and pulled her to the end of the bed. He pulled the lips of her pussy apart and kissed her clit. He looped his tongue around her clit ring, pinched it lightly with his teeth, and sucked away the juices.

Brandon then took his hardened shaft and embedded himself deeply inside her pulsating walls. Bucking and arching and colliding in perfect rhythm, he ground his body into hers.

Lynn moved under him, raising her hips to allow him to dig deeper into her sweetness. "Right there," she said through agonized gasps.

"There?" Brandon asked, fighting for his breath.

Brandon lifted her hips to his thrusting body and continued to rock inside her. He sucked in air through his teeth as he came closer to his climax. He arched and cried her name. "Lynn, Lynn . . . Damn! I love you, baby."

Brandon groaned in bliss as his seed spilled into her. He grabbed Lynn's face and covered her with kisses as he took three last hard pumps into her tight depths. He pulled out of her sweetness, and demanded that she sit on his face, so he could please her.

After she straddled his face and lowered herself down on top of him, he grabbed her hips and held them tight and sucked and bit her clit.

Lynn released in a wave of convulsions. She lay down next to Brandon, and he grabbed her tight. He kissed her on the forehead, and they lay in silence, both wishing that tomorrow would never come.

# Chapter 8

## Wanted

When Chris drove up in front of the building, Shawn was sitting on the steps in the chilly January air, his head in his hands. He hadn't been home in a couple days and he knew that him being on the steps meant trouble. He hadn't called Shawn to tell him he wasn't coming home. He was a grown man and reserved the right to stay out as he liked. *Here we go with the tantrum shit*, Chris thought to himself. He knew Shawn would bitch and moan about it.

"What you doing out here?" Chris asked, his left foot resting on the bottom step.

Shawn lifted his head to look at him. "They took everything."

"Who took everything?" Chris stared at Shawn in confusion. He was sure Shawn was going to start acting a fool, but he was seriously taken by surprise. "What are you talking about?"

Shawn moved to the side for Chris to pass. "Go see for yourself."

Chris walked past him and up the steps to the front door of the building. When he reached the top of the steps on the second floor, the door to his room was laying on the floor as if someone had knocked it down.

He pulled his gun out of the back of his pants and cocked it as a precaution, and proceeded down the hall with it by his side. Approaching the doorway, Chris lifted the gun from his side and aimed it straight ahead. He stepped over the door and entered the room, his gun still drawn.

After searching every corner of the room with his eyes, he finally lowered his gun and tucked it back in his pants. He looked at the mess that lay all over his room. His mattress lay halfway off the bed and was cut open, like they were looking for some cash. Chris wasn't concerned about them finding his stash; it was almost impossible.

He moved the bed and felt around for the permanent black scuff mark he'd put there with his boots. He knelt down and loosened the floorboard. He removed it and stuck his hand down inside the hollow hole he'd created when he moved in.

*Naw, this ain't right,* Chris thought to himself. Only two muthafuckas knew where he kept his money, and that was him and Shawn.

Chris had over one hundred grand stashed under that floor panel. It wouldn't be nothing to make the money back on the street, but he still wanted to know who had enough heart to run up in him like this. He got up from the floor and stormed back down the steps and out the front door to where Shawn still sat with his head in his hands.

Chris grabbed him up from the steps by his neck and looked him in the eye. "You told them where my cash was?" Chris bit on his lip, as he did every time when he was upset.

"They threatened to kill me," Shawn said, a look of terror on his face.

Shawn shook uncontrollably. He didn't know what was worse, facing Chris about the whole situation or dying at the hands of a bunch of ruthless thieves. Believe it or not, he was actually thinking about letting them kill him.

Chris squeezed his neck a little tighter. "Who threatened to kill you?"

"The guy wearing the ski mask," Shawn said, choking on his saliva.

"How many of them was it?"

"Three."

"What else did they take?"

"A couple pounds of weed and a ki of coke."

Chris yelled at the top of his lungs, "Shit!" It was definitely going to take some time to make his money back, especially now that both his money and product were gone. He let go of Shawn. "What did they look like?"

"I don't know. They had on ski masks. One did have a tattoo of a skull with a sword through it on his forearm."

"Oh, yeah?"

"Yeah. He was the one calling all the shots."

Chris pulled Shawn inside the vestibule. "Go stay at your mom's for the night. I'll call you when I get home."

"But—"

"Just do what I say."

Chris left out of the vestibule and got back into the stolen car he used to go meet Tracy. He reached under the dash and started it up with the wires, just as he did before. Then he drove off, headed toward the projects to see his man Black, the eyes and ears of the projects. If something was going down, Black knew what it was. His information never came cheap though.

Chris flipped through the wad of cash he had in his jean pocket. It was a cool grand there. Enough to at least get a name out of him.

He parked the car around the corner from the Blum and hustled up the sidewalk to the buildings. He pulled his hoodie over his head to conceal his face and made his way past the housing cops. He rode the elevator up to the fourth floor and traveled to the end of the hallway, where Black's apartment was located. He knocked on the door and waited for him to answer.

Black cracked the door open, the chain still in place. He smiled through the small opening. "Aww shit! What's up, Chief?"

"Nigga, let me in."

Black closed his door back to unlatch the chain and then let Chris in.

Walking into the apartment, there was a thick cloud of smoke surrounding the entire living room, as if Black had been blazing for days. Chris noticed a blunt smoking in the ashtray. He immediately picked it up and took a long drag. He sat down at the kitchen table and watched as Black threw the dice on the table.

"So what can I do for you, homie?" Black asked, continuing to throw the dice on the table.

"I need a little info." Chris finished off the blunt and smothered it out in the ashtray.

"What's that?" Black asked, chewing on a drinking straw.

"I need to know who ran up in my crib tonight." Chris pulled the grand out of his pocket and placed it on the table. He then slid it in Black's direction.

Black grabbed the money and counted it out. He then lay it back on the table and gave Chris a crazy smirk. "Word on the street is, a lot of niggas want ya head." Black chewed on the straw.

"Oh really?" Chris leaned back in his chair.

"You know what, Chief? I ain't gonna even hold you. That nigga De'Andre had some niggas run up in ya crib."

Chris's right eyebrow rose. He pushed himself away from the table and got up. He shook Black's hand. "Thanks for the info, man." He left out the door.

Chris was going to handle De'Andre in his own time. He

had other issues to deal with, like finding a new crib. He wasn't concerned about making his money back because he knew when he went for De'Andre, he was gonna take everything he had, including his life.


Even after four days Chris still hadn't made it back to the hospital. It wasn't that he didn't care about his mother; it was just that there was money to be made. He spent several days checking on his money and making sure everything was straight. After letting De'Andre go, Chris decided that he would no longer trust anyone to pick up his money. He would take care of that, and if it meant being out all night, then that's what he had to do.

He also made a few phone calls and found himself another place to stay, moving over to 18th and Master Street in a one-bedroom apartment.

Chris hadn't heard from or seen De'Andre, but the info Black gave him made him keep a hammer on his hip. If De'Andre was bold enough to run up in his spot, then he may be stupid enough to try something else.


Chris arrived home from taking care of business. He kicked his boots off at the door and dropped his Nike duffel bag with last week's profit beside them. He placed his gun and cell phone on top of the TV stand and continued taking off the rest of his clothes. He noticed his cell phone was beeping. He flipped it open, and there was a missed call from a number he had never seen before.

He dialed into voice mail and pressed 1, to play the message. He dropped the phone to the floor in disbelief, causing Shawn to jump up from the bed.

"What going on?" Shawn asked, rubbing his eyes.

"It's-it's-its my mom."

"What about her?"

"She's . . . she's . . . " Chris's voice trailed off.

"She's what?"

Chris sat down on the bed. "She's dead."

"What do you mean, she's dead?"

"Ms. Ethel just called and said she passed away almost two hours ago." Chris tried to hide his tears by acting as if he was rubbing his eyes.

Shawn didn't know what he should say, so he remained silent.

"I gotta go to the hospital." Chris got up from the bed and stepped into his boots. He then proceeded out the door and didn't look back.


When Chris arrived at the hospital, Ms. Ethel and Brandon were sitting in the empty room where his mother's body once laid.

Brandon, his eyes deeply saddened, looked up at Chris as he entered the room. "She's gone, man."

"What happened?" Chris said, looking toward the both of them for answers.

"She had a massive heart attack," Ms. Ethel said between sobs. "None of the doctors saw it coming. She was doing well, and then all of a sudden, it happened."

Chris backed out of the room. *She's not dead. They're lying to me.*

"Son, wait." Ms. Ethel held her hands out for him to come and join her and Brandon by the bed. "Come pray with us," she said, bending down on her knees in front of the empty hospital bed.

Chris shook his head and rushed down the hall to the elevators. He looked back in the direction of the room and saw Brandon walking behind him. He began running down the hospital corridor. He pressed the button for the elevator and waited anxiously for it to come. He looked over his shoulder, and Brandon was less than ten feet away. He watched the light flash at his floor and mumbled to himself, "Hurry up, hurry up, hurry up."

The doors opened, and he hurried on just as Brandon was about to reach out for him. He slumped down to the floor on the empty elevator and folded his hands in the prayer position. He rocked back in forth and mumbled to himself again. "Please, God, make this go away. Give me my mom back."

It rained so hard the day of Ms. Ruth's funeral, Chris felt like God was punishing him. He had taken his mother from him and wouldn't even allow him to give her a sunny homecoming. Chris sat silently in the first pew of the First Baptist Church of Germantown in a daze. He listened with open ears as the choir began to sing "Soon and Very Soon." Even though he was wide-awake, he felt like he was in a bad dream.

It was now his turn to view the body for the last time. He made his way out of the pew and prooceded up the aisle to see his mother for the last time. Tears streamed down his face as he stared at the cream casket before him.

Ms. Ruth looked so peaceful to Chris in her navy blue-and-white suit that she wore to service on holidays, and a pair of white gloves to match. Her hair was pent back in a French roll, and her finest church hat was placed neatly on top.

Chris touched her hand, which felt ice-cold. "Momma!" he cried out, throwing himself over her body.

The entire congregation watched in horror as he tried to lift her out of the coffin.

Brandon eased himself out of his seat beside Tracy and hurried to the front of the church. He took a deep breath and grabbed Chris's arm. At first, he wouldn't budge, but after a tender tug, he laid her peacefully back into the coffin and rested in Brandon's embrace.

Brandon never thought he and Chris would come together, and at a time like this made it even more unbelievable to him. He patted Chris on the back. "It's going to be okay, man."

Chris finally looked up at Brandon, but for the first time in a long time, his eyes were warm and full of sorrow. Seeing his mother laid up in a casket made him realize that he needed to make some changes in his life or he was sure to be lying in a casket himself sometime soon.

Brandon held his arm tight and led him back to his seat, where he drooped back down in the pew and held his head in his hands.

Tracy crossed over to the pew where Chris was sitting and sat beside him. She lifted his head from out of his hands and wiped his face with a tissue she pulled from her bag. "Everything's going to be fine." She rubbed his back. "She's in a better place now."

Chris watched solemnly as the pallbearers carried his mother's casket out of the church. The church was almost cleared out, but he was yet to move out of his seat. He sat there staring at the picture of Jesus that rested on the church wall.

Tracy still sat beside him, hoping to ease his pain.

"Why did you have to take her? Why?" he asked, staring at the portrait.


After the funeral, Chris sat in the living room of his mother's home and picked at a plate of food Tracy had made for him. His appetite was shot, and all he could think about was how he was going to survive without her. He sat quietly, oblivious to his surroundings, and continued to question what his life would be like after today.

Ms. Ethel took a seat next to Chris on the couch and patted his leg. "Everything's going to be all right, baby," she said.

Tears streamed down into Chris's plate as he continued to pick at the piece of chicken, which was now cold. *No, everything's not going to be all right.* He started sobbing harder.

Ms. Ethel took the plate out of his hands and placed it on the coffee table in front of him and then took him into her arms. "There, there, baby. I promise you, everything will be okay." She handed him a tissue and waited for him to dry his eyes. She then pulled a small envelope from the drawer of the side table beside her and handed it to him.

"What's this?" Chris sniffled as he looked at the envelope with his name written in cursive.

"Your mother asked me to give this to you if something ever happened to you."


When Tracy got in from the funeral service, it was late in the evening. After helping Ms. Ethel clean up and making sure Chris was okay, she'd had a long day.

She opened the door to their two-story home and closed it back carefully, hoping not to wake Hakeem and Li'l Chris. She placed her purse and jacket on the table by the door and took her heels off and carried them in her hand. She opened the vestibule door and saw Hakeem and Li'l Chris laid out on the sofa in the living room, with the TV playing very soft.

Tracy's plan was to sneak past Hakeem and up to the bedroom then say she'd been home for hours ago, but Hakeem caught her halfway up the steps, grabbing her by her ponytail and dragging her down the steps, making sure that the back of her head felt each bump.

By the time she got down to the last step, Tracy prayed to God that she would just pass out.


"Where you been all this time? Huh?" Hakeem asked, her ponytail firmly in grip.

"I was at the house cleaning up after the wake."

"No, you wasn't. Tell me the truth. You was fucking that nut-ass baby daddy of yours, wasn't you?" Hakeem grasped her hair even tighter.

Tracy looked at Li'l Chris, who was sitting up on the couch, a horrified expression on his face.

Hakeem yelled, "Bitch, I know you heard me!" He let go of her hair, allowing her head to hit the hardwood floor.

He went over to the closet, took out his cowhide leather belt, and wrapped it around his hand. "That's okay. You don't have to tell me. I'm going to beat it out of you." He swung it to her face.

"Please don't do this," Tracy pleaded from a fetal position.

Hakeem continued hitting her over and over again, all the while smiling. When Li'l Chris began to cry for his mother, he stopped and gave him a stern look. "Shut that shit up 'fore I come over there and give you something to cry for."

He turned his attention back to Tracy, who was lying limp on the floor beside his legs. He kicked her in the chest, and she coughed up blood. "Are you going to answer me? Or do I have to keep going?" He hit her one more time across the shoulders with his belt.

Tracy remained silent, hoping he would leave her alone. Of all the beatings he'd given her, this was definitely the worst.

Li'l Chris screamed out again, and Hakeem stopped what he was doing and walked over to the couch. He grabbed Li'l Chris by his shirt. "Didn't I tell you to shut the fuck up?"

With a sudden burst of energy, Tracy got up from the floor and quickly scanned the room for the first thing she could use as a weapon. "No!" Tracy wailed, picking up the lamp on the side table and hitting Hakeem on the head with it.

"Arghhh!" He let go of Li'l Chris and charged Tracy. "You fucking bitch!"

Tracy stood firm and waited for Hakeem's 250-pound body to knock her to the ground. She felt herself being pounded in the head with his fist and prayed to God that, if He allowed her to live through this one, she would leave him and never come back.

# Chapter 9

## Saint Valentine

It was noon when Brandon returned home from Lynn's house. He didn't plan on spending the night out, but after they made love, he didn't feel right leaving her alone. This was the third time he'd stayed out all night to be with her. He also felt guilty for staying out all night because he missed his baby girl.

Brandon opened the door to the apartment and locked it behind himself. Before he could do anything else, he went back to the nursery to check on Kai.

When he'd opened the door, Mia was sitting in the rocking chair by the crib with the baby in her arms. This made him feel even guiltier. She looked up at him and then back down at the baby.

Brandon's eyes bulged as he noticed the black-and-blue marks around her neck where he had gripped her up. His wife had driven him to become a monster. He couldn't stand to look at her any longer, so he closed the door and made his way back to the kitchen.

He placed his keys on the marble kitchen countertop and headed straight for the fridge to grab a cold beer. He popped the top off, took a long swig, and closed the door to the refrigerator. He then proceeded to the couch, where he took off his Prada sneakers and stretched out.

He flipped on the news and began to nod off. The night he had with Lynn was so explosive, he didn't get much sleep.

"I'm sorry, baby," Mia said, moving his feet and taking a seat next to him on the couch. "I promise, no more late nights."

Mia's apology was a step in the right direction, but Brandon still felt as though their marriage was heading in the wrong direction. He pecked her on the lips and continued to flip through the channels.

"What the hell kind of kiss was that? I want a real kiss."

The phone rang just as Mia jumped into his lap and started to kiss on his face.

"Hello," Brandon said, pushing her away.

"Mr. Brunson, there's a woman down here in the lobby asking for a Tifah," the front desk attendant said. "She claims that this woman lives in your apartment. I told her that no such person lives in this building, but she insisted that I call you."

"There's no Tifah here."

"Well, from the description she gave me, it seems like it might be your wife."

"Hold on for a minute."

Brandon looked over at Mia and held the phone out. "Uhmmm . . . babe, the front desk." He became suspicious. The name sounded familiar. He just couldn't recall where or when he'd heard it.

Mia took the phone from Brandon, clicked it off, and placed it on the coffee table.  "I'll just go down to the lobby and see what's going on." She jumped up from the couch and walked out the door.

Mia's face turned a bright red as she walked down the hall-way to the elevators. *This can't be happening,* she thought as the elevator arrived. When she got down to the lobby, the front desk attendant had the woman pulled over to the side, so the other residents and visitors could still be serviced.

She smiled faintly at the front desk attendant before grabbing the woman by the arm and snatching her away into the mailroom. She closed the door and leaned against it. "What the hell are you doing here?" Mia snarled.

Mia looked her over at the light-skinned woman in a headscarf and tattered blue jeans. She had on a red leather jacket with a white T-shirt beneath it and a pair of brown penny loafers with no socks, although it was 38 degrees outside, and there was snow on the ground from a storm that passed two days ago.

"I need to borrow a couple dollars." The woman ground her teeth together.

"Didn't I tell you never to come around here?"

"Tifah, please . . . I ain't eat in three days. I'm hungry."

"Don't call me that. That's not my name. How I know you ain't gonna spend it on crack?"

"I give you my word, Tifah—I mean Mia." She held her hand up like a Girl Scout.

Mia dug into her pocket and pulled out a crisp fifty-dollar bill. "Here, Mom. If I find out you bought crack with it, I'll never give you another dime. And don't come 'round here no more."

"I promise, Tifah, I won't." She looked at the crispy bill in her hands. "Thanks, baby."

"Now get out of here."

Mia stepped out of the doorway, allowing her to pass by her. Mia held her nose as she passed. She smelled of cheap booze, sweat, and crack, of course. Mia was the spitting image of her mother, but most people couldn't make it out because her mother had smoked her looks away years ago.

She waited for her to leave out the door before leaving the mailroom. She tried to bypass the front desk attendant and head straight for the elevators, but he noticed her just as she passed the desk.

"Mrs. Brunson."

Mia rolled her eyes and turned back around toward the desk. She put on the friendliest smile she could muster. "Yes?"

"Did you know that woman?" he said, raising an eyebrow.

"Oh, she's just some homeless woman I gave change to before. I guess she followed me home." Mia smiled.

He smiled back. "You're such a humanitarian."

"I try," she said, flashing her fake smile again. "Can you do me a favor? The next time she comes in here, could you make sure that you tell her I no longer live here. I don't want every bag lady I give change to come seeking me out at my home."

"No problem, Ms. Brunson. I'll make sure she doesn't step another foot on the premises."

"Thank you." Mia placed a twenty in his hand.

Mia walked over to the elevator and waited for it to arrive. Once on board, she let out a long sigh. Her mom coming to their condo building was just too close for comfort. Luckily she was home to catch her before she got to Brandon.

Mia hardly spoke with her mother or anyone else in her family. They were ghetto people who sat around and collected welfare. She would rather die than have her name associated with them. That's exactly why she changed her name. She couldn't see herself walking around for the rest of her life as some Latifah. She was too sexy for that name. So when she turned eighteen, she changed her name and never looked back.

When Mia got back in the house, Brandon was sitting in the nursery feeding the baby. *I swear, sometimes I think he loves that damn baby more than he does me.* She watched from afar as he placed Kai on his shoulder to burp her. He patted her on the back and continued rocking her until she fell asleep. Mia thought having Kai was an investment, but she was becoming more of a replacement. She had to do something about the bond they shared. He never seemed to care much about anything, but when Kai came along all that changed. *Maybe I could get an around-the-clock nanny. That way Brandon never has to watch after her.*

Brandon kissed Kai on the forehead and placed her carefully in the crib. She was growing so fast now. At six months, Kai looked more like a one-year-old. Her chubby cheeks protruded from her face, and her smile melted Brandon's heart every time. He stood by the crib and watched her sleep. She was the best thing he'd ever done with his life. Kai meant the world to him. She was the reason why he agreed to remain civil with Chris. Brandon decided that the beef between the two of them was too risky; he wanted to be around for his baby girl when she needed him.

He sat back down in the rocking chair to catch a nap. The last thing he wanted to do was go lie down in the bedroom and have Mia bug him about where he was last night. He'd rather be in the company of his little princess anyway. She loved him, and unlike Mia, she couldn't lie to him.

Ever since New Year's, Mia seemed to take more interest in her family, which gave Brandon less time to be with Lynn. He didn't mind though. It seemed that his perfect family was finally starting to take shape, and he embraced it. He didn't completely forget about Lynn. He texted her daily and always made it his business to at least get in a weekly phone call. She didn't seem upset that he was unable to spend time with her; in fact she seemed to be quite busy herself.

Mia was definitely starting to play her part, fucking him on the daily basis and even trying to cook for him. He sat through her disastrous meals with a smile on his face all because she was making an effort.

Just last night she tried her hand at baking apple pie. Now, the crust was burnt and the apples a little sour, but hey, in his book she made it with love. They spent their days out and about taking Kai to the park, and their nights cuddled up on the couch. Mia was actually being a wife, and in Brandon's book, she was claiming her man and her family.

Brandon got up early on Valentine's Day in a state of panic. Today was his one-year wedding anniversary, and he hadn't bought her anything, not even a card. It wasn't that he forgot to buy Mia a present. He just didn't know what to get her. *What do you get for someone who has everything and not break the bank?* Brandon thought to himself.

Mia had been hinting at this diamond circle pendant from Tiffany & Company. He didn't want to spend that much. Five grand was a lot of money, given the state of their financial situation. He was down to fifty thousand dollars in the bank, and his twenty-five hundred dollar mortgage payment was due at the end of the week. Knowing that if he didn't get it, he would never hear the last of it, he drove down to their Walnut Street store location and parked his car with the valet.

When he entered the store, there were several sales reps waiting to serve him. Ignoring the young black girl who said hello, he stopped in front of a middle-aged white woman with curly reddish-brown hair. Nothing against his race, but whenever he purchased expensive items, Brandon would rather deal with the white man. He had his credit card stolen the last time he sought help from a black store associate.

"Hello, sir." The woman smiled warmly. "How can I help you?"

"I'm looking for a gift for my wife," Brandon said, leaning on the glass counter. "It's our anniversary." He dug into his pocket and took out the page from the Tiffany's catalog that Mia had left on his pillow every day for a week. "I have a picture of it right here."

"Oh, yes, sir. I know exactly what you are talking about." She reached into the display case and returned with the Victoria pendant.

"This is a lovely necklace, sir. It's set with our most glamorous Tiffany diamonds. And let's not forget the cultured pearls set in platinum. Your wife will be very happy with this piece."

Brandon's stomach soured as he looked at the price tag—$5,300. He knew it cost about five stacks, but knowing and paying for it was two different things. "I don't even want to look at it," he said, pulling his wallet out of his pants pocket. "Just wrap it up and charge my card." He handed the sales associate his American Express black card. He stood at the glass case admiring a pair of diamond-encrusted cufflinks while the sales associate went over to the register area to run his card.

The clerk returned from the cash register. "Mr. Brunson, I'm sorry, but your card was denied."

Trying not to lose his cool, Brandon gave off a look of concern. "That can't be possible."

"I'm sorry, Mr. Brunson. I can't accept this card. Do you have any other method of payment? We take cash, checks, or maybe you have another credit card." She placed his black card on the glass countertop in front of him.

Brandon grabbed his card and placed it back into his wallet, trying his damnedest not to cause a scene about his card being denied. It had to be a mistake on their part, because he paid his bill faithfully on the first of each month. As soon as he left out of the store, he planned to give the card company a call. He searched the small section behind his ID and found the blank check he always kept in case of an emergency. Before writing it out, he decided to go with a more affordable piece of jewelry.

Brandon looked at the clerk's name tag. "Kathy, would you be a darling and find me a nice necklace but at half the price?"

"Sure, Mr. Brunson, not a problem." Kathy took the $5,300 necklace out of the box and restocked it in the case. She searched the case and then reached for another necklace. "This is our heart pendant with pink sapphires and round brilliant diamonds. It's set in platinum." She held it out for him to see.

Brandon took the necklace into his hands and examined it closely. It was just okay to him. It wasn't as nice as the one that she really wanted, but it would do. Usually, he would be more concerned about the presentation of the piece, but this time around, he worried about the price. He peeped at the price tag—$1,800. He handed it back to her and nodded in affirmation.

While Kathy packed the necklace up in a box, he wrote out the check, and when she was done, he handed it to her.

Brandon tapped impatiently on the glass counter as he waited for her to ring up the purchase. She returned with the receipt and placed the wrapped gift in his hand. He placed the finely wrapped box in the inside pocket of his brown Kenneth Cole leather bomber jacket and zipped it up to face the cold February winds.

He left out of the store and picked up his car from the valet. He hurried over to his condo, which was only four blocks over and parked the car. Mia had told him that she was treating her mother to a late Valentine's Day lunch so she wouldn't be back for at least a couple of hours. He wanted to make the call to the credit card company before she got in. Something told him she had a lot to do with his card being denied.


Brandon slammed the phone down on the American Express card services representative. Mia had managed to run up a whopping $25,000 in purchases in a matter of a weekend, and they shut the card off as a precaution.

Brandon had never spent that type of money in such a short amount of time. His mind was still boggled as to where the money was going. He'd been checking Mia's closet daily for new items and hadn't seen anything in over a month. After having a long serious talk about the state of their finances, she seemed to get the hint, but his credit card being denied only told him that she had become craftier in hiding her spending habits. He decided to keep his suspicions to himself for the time being. He knew Mia was up to no good, but he wanted to focus on trying to have a good evening with her.

He placed the long-stemmed yellow roses he'd ordered in a crystal vase in the middle of the coffee table. He then lit several scented candles around their condo, from the kitchen to the bedroom. Brandon was lucky enough to score the head chef of Vetri Ristorante, one of Mia's favorite eateries, to prepare a gourmet meal in their home for dinner. It cost him five hundred dollars, but he realized he had to compensate for the cheap present.

Brandon scurried about the house, tidying up, and then went on to get ready for dinner. He'd paid the nanny for the entire night, so they could enjoy some alone time. He set the kitchen counter with their finest porcelain china and crystal champagne flutes. A bottle of Moët sat chilling in an ice bucket, and R. Kelly's 12 Play thumped from the stereo. Mia loved R. Kelly, so Brandon was sure to get some ass tonight.

Mia walked in the door at seven p.m. sharp. Brandon looked her over as she stopped at the couch to lay down her bag. She had on a black Loro Piana chinchilla-collared cashmere cape, which she bought at her last shopping spree at Bergdorf Goodman, and a pair of black patent leather Manolo Blahnik shoes to match. When she threw her cape across the back of the sofa, she revealed a purple multicolor geometric print Emilio Pucci dress.

Brandon stood by as she strutted into the bathroom and returned five minutes later. She walked up to him, and he took her by the waist and gave her a long, inviting kiss.

"You missed me, huh?"

Mia broke away from him as her nose embraced the smell of her favorite Italian dish, eggplant ravioli with smoked mozzarella. She walked around him and headed for the kitchen counter. She picked through her plate and nibbled on a piece of eggplant. Sitting down at the counter, Mia draped her napkin in her lap and waited for Brandon to seat himself.

Brandon opened up the bottle of Moët he had chilling on ice and poured two glasses. He placed one in front of Mia and sat down across from her.

"To love," Mia said dryly, raising her glass to toast.

Brandon lifted his glass. "To love."

They both took a sip from their glasses and went back to eating in silence.

Brandon twirled his spaghetti around his fork and stuffed it in his mouth. He looked over at Mia, who seemed to be occupied with her own plate of food. He had grown to love her, but he knew it wasn't going to work out. She was too worldly for him. He needed a family-oriented person in his life, and that was definitely Lynn.

As he took another sip of his champagne, he wondered what Lynn was doing at that very moment. He almost made himself mad, thinking she might be with another man.

Mia finished off her plate and patted her mouth with her napkin. She looked over at Brandon, and he still had half of his food left. He looked sad, almost as if he would rather be somewhere else. Mia knew he was probably thinking about Lynn. She didn't care though. In a few more months, both of them would be obsolete in her eyes.

She'd had lunch with Lynn earlier today for Valentine's

Day and bought her the cutest little diamond stud earrings from Macy's. She couldn't wait until her plan took full action. Brandon would shit himself when he found out his precious Lynn was a carpet-muncher. Last week, she tried Lynn, and even though she had never had a woman before, that didn't stop her from being curious.

Mia ate her phat, juicy pussy like it was going out of style, and Lynn had been blowing her phone up ever since. Eating pussy wasn't nothing new to Mia. Her and her girlfriend Sam used to eat each other out all the time when they were in college.

Brandon finally finished his food and cleared the kitchen counter of all the dishes. He sat down beside Mia who had kicked her shoes off and was now reading a *Vogue* magazine. He placed the neatly wrapped Tiffany's box in her lap and she threw the magazine to the floor.

"Did you get it?" she asked. She squealed like a child as she pulled the ribbon loose.

Hoping that she would like the gift, Brandon stood silent and braced himself for her response. When she pulled the top off and noticed it wasn't the pendant she wanted, her smile turned into a frown.

"I can tell by the look on your face that you don't like it."

"It's . . . nice." She examined every detail as she held it in her hands.

"I'll take it back in the morning." Brandon took it from her and placed it back in its box.

"No, no, no. Don't do that," Mia said, forcing a smile. She placed the necklace around her neck and went over to look at herself in the wall mirror. She wouldn't be caught dead in such a hideous piece of jewelry, but what the hell, it was a holiday and she didn't feel like fighting.

"So what did you get me?"

"The same thing I got you last year—a wet pussy and a lean back." She stepped out of her dress and revealed a skimpy see-through bra and thong set. Her perky nipples peeped through the bra, and her round, supple ass stood at attention as she twirled around and gave him the back view.

Brandon's wood shot up in no time.

The last thing Mia wanted to do was give him some ass, but she felt obligated because he bought her that tacky necklace, which she would most likely never wear again after tonight.

She closed her eyes and sighed. *Let the games begin*, she thought, as he pried her legs apart and entered her roughly.

# Chapter 10

## Raw, Rough, and Rugged
## Chris

Chris sat slumped down in the recliner chair in front on the television staring at the sealed envelope Ms. Ethel gave him the day of his mother's funeral. It had been four months since her death, and Mother's Day was approaching. He ripped open the envelope and unfolded the letter. As he began reading, he could hear his mother's voice as if she was actually having a conversation with him.

My loving son Chris,

I know I may not have always been the best mother, but I wanted you to know that I tried my best to raise you to be a responsible, God-fearing man. I'm sorry, Chris. I'm sorry that I allowed you to be hurt and I stood by and did nothing about it. I didn't know what to do or what to say. I just thought that if I never mentioned it, it would go away. I lived with the regret of not doing anything about it for the rest of my days, and I want you to know that I too hurt. I hurt because I allowed a man to take my son's innocence away. In my heart, I knew I was wrong, but I just didn't know how to deal with it. I don't want you to think that this apology is an excuse for my actions because it's not. I just want you to know that, as your mother, I should have stood up for you and made him pay for what he did. Thank you for being my son and loving me regardless of my mistakes. Remember, I will always love you no matter what.

Mom

Chris wiped at his eyes with the bottom of his T-shirt. He folded the letter back up and placed it neatly back in the envelope as if he'd never opened it. He then went over to the dresser drawer and placed it in the very back, behind his socks and underwear. He sat back down in the recliner.

Shawn walked up behind Chris and placed his hand on his shoulder. He began to massage his neck. He went in for a kiss, but Chris swatted him away.

"You okay?"

Chris pushed Shawn's hand off his shoulder. "I'm good. I just need some time to myself. Why don't you go stay at ya mom's crib for a while?"

Shawn didn't have the energy to argue with Chris, so he nodded and grabbed his Luis Vuitton duffel bag from the closet. He packed enough clothes to last him the entire weekend.

Lately, Chris had been taking the death of his mother out on Shawn. If he wasn't fucking Shawn, then they had nothing in common. Their sex became more aggressive to the point where Shawn had to be hospitalized for a week for a ripped anus. The only reason he was still around was because of his cousin De'Andre, and of course, the cash. De'Andre told him that if he broke up with Chris, he would lose his spot as his head drug dealer. So Shawn promised De'Andre he would stick around for a few months, but after that, he was on his own. De'Andre agreed that all he needed was a few months to put his plan into place.

Plus, Chris wasn't coming up off the dough like he was when they'd first met. Shawn had to practically beg the man for ten dollars the other morning, and only after he sucked Chris's dick for a half-hour was he given the money.

"I guess I'll see you later." Shawn threw the duffel bag over his shoulder.

"Yeah, I guess so."

Shawn shook his head and left out of the door. Whatever De'Andre had planned, he needed to hurry up. With Chris being so cold toward him, there was no guarantee they would make it past the month's end.

Just like Chris seemed to be losing interest in Shawn, he was also losing it in him. Shawn closed the front door of the building behind him and took a deep breath. He hadn't stayed at his mother's house since meeting Chris, so this was definitely going to be a change of pace for him. *What the hell*, Shawn thought. *I might as well get used to living away from him now*. He jogged down the steps and walked up the street to the bus stop.

Reading the letter his mother wrote him made Chris angry inside. He secretly hated her for allowing him to suffer all those years without even mentioning what had happened to him. He remembered the look on his mother's face when she walked into the room and saw Mr. Samuel, his stepfather, on top of him. Chris begged her with his eyes to make him stop, but she just turned back around and left out of the room.

It took months for him to be able to look at her in her face after that, and still, she continued to allow him to stay with him. It wasn't until Chris took matters into his own hand and stabbed him in the chest with a knife that he got some relief. He was only ten years old at the time. Ms. Ruth had the nerve to send him away for two years after that because she didn't want the neighbors and the people at their church to find out what was going on.

Chris became a bitter child after that. Feeling like his mom didn't love him, he craved her attention and did whatever he had to do, good or bad, to get it. Chris desperately wanted to

live a regular life, but Mr. Samuel had made him feel like being with a man was normal. He always told Chris that the love
he had for him was normal, and that every man should love
his son the way he loved Chris. When Chris's mother found
out, he just knew it was okay for him to keep doing it to him
because his mother never said it wasn't okay. To Chris, if she
accepted it, then so should he.

Chris got from the chair and searched under the bed for
the half-pound bag of weed he'd bought yesterday from the
Dominicans. He started smoking again to calm his nerves.
Noticing his stash was gone, he started after Shawn, but by
the time he got downstairs, Shawn was nowhere in sight. *That
little muthafucka! I'll deal with him when I see him.*

Chris looked over at the dresser where he placed the letter, and it dawned on him that he had yet to clean out his
mother's house. He grabbed his keys off the top of the top of
the TV and headed out the door without second-guessing his
decision. He got in the car and headed over to his mother's.
He thought about calling Tracy to meet him there. He dialed
her number, but it was disconnected. He hadn't spoken to
her since the last time he was supposed to meet her and she
never showed. He'd asked the few girlfriends she had if they
heard from her, but there was no luck there. Calling her sister
didn't help either. She said that Tracy hadn't called her in
weeks.

Chris was trying to keep his nose clean, but he couldn't
take it any longer. He had a roundabout idea of where the nigga Hakeem sold at, and he had sent some niggas over there to
handle him. He didn't want him dead, but he did want him
close to it. He would have done it himself, but he'd promised
Tracy he would stay out of it.

But he didn't promise her that he wouldn't have somebody
else do the deed. Chris called in a favor to his Dominican

homie, Juan, who said he would handle business and get back with him within the next week.

When Chris pulled up to the house, he noticed Tracy's pearl E-Class parked in the driveway. His heart thudded as he rushed to turn the car off and raced up the stairs to the porch. He quickly fumbled through his keys for the right one and opened the door. It was the first time in a long time Chris had a key to his mother's home. She left the house to him in her will with hopes that he would one day raise his family there.

He opened the door and walked in. He could hear his mother's old clock radio she kept in the kitchen playing the sultry tunes of Mary J. Blige's *No More Drama* softly, instead of the usual gospel music. Chris stood in the walkway between the kitchen and dining room and watched as Tracy bobbed her head and shook her hips as she hummed along with the song.

She stopped in the middle of her tracks as soon as she noticed him staring at her. She turned around and tried to muster a half-smile, but her swollen jaw was wired shut.

Chris rushed over to her and held her so tight, she could hardly breathe. He placed his hand softly on the side of her that was wired shut and kissed her tenderly, allowing his lips to linger on hers. He looked at the stitches over her right eye and the bandage over her nose.

"What happened to you?" he asked, holding her face in his hands.

Tracy quickly pointed to Li'l Chris, who lay knocked out in his Pack & Play crib.

Chris brought his voice down to a much lower decibel. "Sorry."

Knowing she was going to have a hard time trying to talk because of her jaw and all, she decided to go over to her pocketbook in the living room to grab the little legal pad she'd been keeping in there to communicate with people. She sat down at the kitchen table and began writing s few short sentences describing what happened. She decided not to lie this time about Hakeem abusing her, so she told him everything.

Tears of anger flowed from Chris's face after he finished reading the few lines Tracy scribbled on the notepad. *Hakeem has just earned himself a death sentence.* He grabbed Tracy close to his chest and clenched her up in his arms. Seeing the woman he loved hurt was driving him insane.

Tracy couldn't help but to hold him tight. She'd missed him also. After the last fight with Hakeem, she woke up in the intensive care unit of Temple University Hospital. She lied to the staff there and told them that she had gotten into a bad car accident. Hakeem had already threatened that he was going to kill her and her son if anyone found out what really happened. Not taking his threat lightly, Tracy did as she was told.

This last incident left her with a broken jaw, bruised ribs, and thirteen stitches near her eye socket. She was indeed in bad shape, but she would endure the pain again to make sure her son was safe.

Tracy pulled out of his embrace and pressed her lips against his. A chill went up her spine as his lips left her lips and traveled down to her neck. She stood lifeless as his hands explored her hips and thighs. Tracy hadn't felt so good in such a long time, her purple Victoria's Secret thongs were drenched in her juices.

She unbuckled her pants and allowed them to slide down her ankles. She then stepped out of them and twirled around to give Chris the back view of her ass, which was so big and round, he was amazed that it was all hiding in that pair of Seven jeans.

Tracy sauntered up the steps to Chris's old bedroom, where

they had spent several nights together, leaving the jeans in the middle of the kitchen floor.

Chris followed behind her like a little puppy dog, watching her ass bounce as she took each step. He grabbed the crotch of his pants. His member was so swollen, it was starting to ache. It had been some time now since he had been with a woman. After Tracy left him, sex was purely for entertainment. He never enjoyed it with her like he used to because there was no love involved.

She stopped at the door to his old room and leaned against the door, and he placed his arms around her neck and kissed her again. She smiled as much as her jaw would allow her and turned the knob.

Chris walked in behind her, leaving the door open to hear Li'l Chris if he happened to wake up. He sat down on the side of the bed and motioned for her to stand in between his legs. He hugged her tight around the waist and kissed her stomach, which was still nice and tight even after the birth of their son.

Continuing to kiss her belly, Chris slowly worked her purple thongs around her thick thighs and down her ankles, revealing her bushy kitty. He slid off the bed in between her thighs and parted the lips of her pussy with his mouth. He allowed the warmth of his tongue to linger on her clit, before he began stroking her, humming between strokes.

Tracy bit her bottom lip as she remembered how good it felt to have a man tend to her needs. Her legs buckled as he dug deeper into her, forcing his tongue in and out of her hole. Tracy pushed him to the ground, planting her hot wet pussy on top of his face, and began riding him gently as he continued to bite her in all the right places.

"Mmmmm," she moaned, her pussy on Chris's face.

Chris picked up the pace, twirling his tongue in round-about motions.

"Oh, baby, don't stop! I'm about to come," Tracy muttered through her wired jaw, forgetting that the baby was sleep downstairs.

Chris stopped, flipped her over on her back, and buried his head between her legs. He sucked on her pussy until she began screaming his name.

"Oh, Chris! Oh, Chris! Damn, baby!" Tracy was experiencing multiple orgasms.

Keeping her legs parted, Chris slipped his swollen member inside of her with ease and began stroking her, savoring each pleasurable moment.

Tracy grabbed at his back as his swollen rod grabbed at her heated walls, and Chris grabbed her hips and forced all of himself in her, causing her eyes to roll in the back of her head.

"Damn, baby!" Chris heaved. "This pussy is so good."

Lifting her legs higher, Chris dug into her sweetness and began hammering into her petite frame. He took one last pump and blasted into bliss. He then rolled over on his back and tried to catch his breath. His body continued to tingle from the warm sensation of Tracy's pussy engulfing his dick.

Tracy quickly got up from the floor and went into the bathroom to take a shower. She enjoyed Chris's lovemaking, but if Hakeem smelled anything on her that even resembled another man, he would kill her for sure.

After she was finished, she returned to the room and found Chris sleeping peacefully on the bed. She decided to let him rest. She grabbed her clothes, closed the door to the room, and dressed in the hallway.

She then went downstairs to check on Li'l Chris, who was still 'sleep. She gathered her things and loaded up the car. She then picked Li'l Chris up from the couch, closed and locked the front door behind her, and strapped him in his car seat.

As she backed down the driveway, all she could think about

was, she really didn't want to leave. She wanted Chris to protect her and to never leave her side again. She wanted to tell
him that, but she just didn't know how to.

When Chris awoke, it was well into the evening. He looked
at his cell phone and saw there was a missed call from Juan.
He decided to just go and see him.

Chris left out the house, got in the car, and drove over to
5th Street to Juan's barbershop. Juan was just finishing up a
client when he got there, so he took a seat in the waiting area.

Juan came over shortly thereafter. "Chief, what's up?" He
shook Chris's hand. "Let's go in the back and talk."

Chris followed him back into the storage area and took a
seat on a box and folded his hands.

Juan leaned against the water heater. "I sent somebody to
go handle that Hakeem guy. They said the job is done and
that they scared him off."

Chris raised his eyebrow. "Did they make their point clear?"

"Loud and clear."

"Cool." Chris dug into his pockets and returned with five
grand. "Thanks, man," he said, handing him the whack of
cash.

"Anytime, Chief, anytime." Juan placed the whack in his
back pocket.

"I gotta go check on some things. I'll catch up with you
later." Chris got up from the boxes and made his way toward
the front of the barbershop.

"Sure, Chief." Juan waved for the next customer to take a
seat in his chair.

As Chris left out the door and drove off, Hakeem came
barging out of the bathroom stall, his face perfectly intact,
without any scars or bruises. "Juan, my man." He handed him
another whack of cash totaling five grand.

One thing Hakeem knew—When it came to money, niggas were willing to do anything. When Juan's man came to pay him a visit, he'd persuaded him to take the payoff instead.

Juan turned the clippers on. "Hak, remember what we talked about."

"No problem." Hakeem left out, once he made sure the coast was clear.


Chris heard scrambling coming from his room when he hit the top of the stairs of the boarding room. He pulled out his gun and held it down by his side. He eased the key in the lock, turned it quietly, and flung the door wide open, only to find Shawn lying across the chair with his booty in the air and another man digging into his ass.

Shawn jumped up from the chair. "Chris, I-I-I can explain."

Chris just shook his head and backed out of the room. He closed the door and headed back down the steps and out the door. He knew he was over Shawn. If it was any other time, he would have wrung his neck, but after today, he knew what he and Tracy had was real. Chris didn't care about Shawn or no other nigga. His focus was on getting Tracy back, and that required all of his attention.

# Chapter 11

### A Fraud, a Phony, a Fake

### Brandon

Brandon sat at his desk in the living room and looked at this month's bills. It was official. After paying off the mortgage and the car note, he had fifteen thousand dollars left to his name. Upset about his current financial situation, he hurried over to the kitchen cabinet and grabbed a bottle of Seagram's Gin. He opened the top and took a swig right from the bottle. He and Mia needed to have a serious talk. Some of the luxuries they had come accustomed to would now have to become a thing of the past. They already had to let go of the housekeeper and the nanny; they were just too expensive. Brandon had been combing the want ads for a part-time job himself. He felt like the walls were closing in on him; he was once more in the same bind he'd found himself in almost a year ago.

The Fourth of July was less than two weeks away, and he and Mia had plans on spending the holiday in the Hamptons in their time-share. But Brandon already knew that wasn't going to happen, because he had to sell his rental time last week to pay for Mia's new boob job. He begged and pleaded for her to reconsider plastic surgery, but she argued that her career would suffer if she didn't do the procedure. He didn't tell her where the money came from; he just told her it was some investment money he'd put away for rough times. He knew he was due to have the conversation with her about the trip to the Hamptons, but he was too depressed to tackle that issue, which he knew it was going to be.

Brandon was due at a lunch date with Lynn in less than a half-hour. Being the primary babysitter now that the nanny was let go, he hadn't seen her in almost a month.

He took a long shower, shaved, and covered himself with his Issey Miyake cologne. He then slipped on a pair of cream linen shorts and a pink, short-sleeved Polo button-up. He put on his Polo cap, which matched the color of his shorts, and a pair of navy blue Polo skippies to match.

Mia had taken the baby to the doctor's office earlier this morning, so by the time she got back, Brandon would already be gone. He grabbed his keys and made his way down to the lobby area to hail a cab. Mia had their only car, her car, so it was either public transportation or a cab, and Brandon refused to catch the subway and be subjected to bums and crackheads.

Nate, the weekend doorman, waved him over to the front desk. "Mr. Brunson, I was just calling upstairs for you." He placed the phone back on the hook.

"What's up, Nate?" Brandon asked, leaning on the desk. "What can I do for you?"

Nate's eyes shot past Brandon over to the light-skinned woman standing over by the door with a wool coat on and a pair of cowboy boots in the middle of the summer. "That woman over there claims to know your wife." He kept watching the woman with a close eye. "She begged me to call you."

Brandon looked over at the poor woman, who seemed to be going through crack withdrawal. She kept pacing in front of the revolving door, causing it to be in continuous motion. Remembering the incident that took place several months back when a strange woman came to their building looking for Mia, he decided to go over and talk to her.

He walked over to her. "Can I help you? You asked for my wife?"

She looked at Brandon. "Oh, you Tifah husband?"

"I'm sorry. Who did you say?" Brandon said, knowing in his heart that the name sound all too familiar.

The woman hesitated and then decided against pursuing the conversation. "I-I-I . . . " She backed out of the building into the revolving doors, gave a quick wave, and marched up the street as fast as her two feet could take her.

Curious to know more about this mystery woman, Brandon ran out of the building after her to find out who this Tifah person really was. He knew this person had to be related to Mia. He'd seen the name *Latifah* in Mia's personal papers some time ago. He meant to ask her about it, but when he went back to find the papers, they were gone.

"Excuse me! Miss!" Brandon said, walking swiftly behind her. He wasn't trying to lose her in the lunchtime rush hour.

She looked back at Brandon, who was gaining on her, and started moving faster. She finally found her way inside one of the office buildings, leaving Brandon behind.

He stood on the corner of the block and tried to spot the direction in which she went. *It couldn't be that hard to find her. She had on a wool coat in the summer, for Christ's sake.* He checked two of the buildings, but there was no sign of her. There was definitely something fishy going on.

Placing the thoughts of the women in the back of his mind, Brandon regained focus and hailed a cab to Lynn's house.

He passed by the front desk attendant with ease and made his way up to her apartment. He knocked lightly at the door and waited for her to answer. Starting to get impatient, Brandon knocked again, but this time with a little more force.

***

"I'm coming!" Lynn scrambled around the room for her clothes.

Lynn looked over at Nina, who was still lying on the bed naked with a frantic look on her face. When Nina stopped past unexpectedly this morning, she quickly forgot all about her and Brandon's lunch date. Her soft kisses continued to dance in Lynn's mind as she tried to gather herself.

"Get dressed." She threw Mia's underwear at her.

Mia rolled her eyes as she stepped into her panties and pulled them up around her waist. She grabbed her bra and her Dolce & Gabbana sundress from the floor and put them on also.

"Fuck him." Mia grabbed Lynn by the waist and pulled her close. She kissed her, sucking on her bottom lip.

Lynn returned the kiss and pulled away. "I promised him I would go to lunch with him."

Looking at Lynn's naked body one last time, Mia decided to try something else. She waited for Lynn to bend down to grab her underwear and then came up behind her and began licking her kitty with long, wet strokes.

A chill spilled through Lynn's body, and Mia's full lips suckled her clit with a force of a vacuum, causing Lynn's knees to buckle.

"Please. You have to go." Lynn moved in the direction of the bed.

Lynn didn't really want her to go. Nina had made her feel like no man had ever made her. Being with a woman was such a new world to Lynn that every touch made her excited. With such a gorgeous woman interested in her, it had been hard for her to focus. She found herself engrossed in Nina's every movement.

Brandon leaned against the door and heard muffled

sounds, but he couldn't make out any words. Lynn was beginning to piss him off. He had reservations at the Bridget Foy's,
her favorite restaurant, and they were already a half-hour late.

He banged on the door even harder. "What the hell are
you doing in there?" He turned the knob to see if the door
was open, and to his amazement, it swung open. "Lynn!"

Lynn jumped up off the bed and led Mia to the bedroom
closet. "Stay here until I leave." She closed the door in a hurry. She stood in the middle of the bedroom naked and waited
for Brandon to come busting in, which she knew he was going
to do without a doubt.

Seconds later, he eased the door open and peeked in. He
was delighted to see that she wasn't wearing any clothing.
Licking his lips in his delight, he placed his arms around her
neck and pecked her on the lips. "What's taking you so long?"
he asked, looking into her eyes.

"I was just trying to figure out what outfit I wanted to
wear." Lynn placed her arms around his waist and tiptoed to
peck him on the lips

Just then he noticed a diamond necklace around her neck
similar to the one he gave Mia for Valentine's Day. He carefully lifted the pendant from her chest and held it in his hands.
"Where did you get this?" He brought it closer to his face.

"A friend gave it to me as a gift."

Brandon raised an eyebrow. "A friend, huh. That's an expensive necklace. Anyone who spends that type of money on
you is definitely more than a friend." He released the pendant. He made a mental note to check Mia's jewelry box at
home for the pendant he'd bought her.

Brandon smacked her on the butt. "Get dressed. By the
time we get to the restaurant, we won't get a table at all."

"I'll be out in a minute." She closed the door and locked it
behind him. Then she ran over to the closet and opened the
door.

Mia sat on the closet floor, in her underwear, her hands folded. It took everything out of her not to jump out of that closet and bust Brandon right then and there. She remained calm and grabbed her shoes from the bedroom floor. In a few weeks, this whole shenanigan would be over, and Brandon would be at her mercy.

Brandon did exactly what she wanted him to do—Notice the pendant. This would only be the first of several little booby traps she set for him.

After months of planning, things were finally in place and running just the way she wanted them to. She had Lynn eating out of her hands, which was the hardest part. Now, all she had to do was make sure her new place was ready for her, and after talking to her real estate agent, she'd found out that it would be ready in less than no time.

Lynn grabbed the first thing she came across in her closet, a pair of dark blue Old Navy jeans and a tube top. She put on her black high-heeled Aldo sandals with the rhinestones across the front and brushed her hair back in a simple ponytail.

Mia almost threw up when she saw the ensemble. *You think she would have at least learned to be a little stylish, hanging with me.* She shook her head and peered through the open vents in the closet door.


Out of all the things that seemed to going wrong in his life, the one thing that was going right for Brandon was the fact that he was back to being the Brandon he used to be physically that is. Last week, he got word from his doctor that he no longer needed his cane, and he hadn't used it since. He couldn't wait for Lynn to see he was back to his old self. He even went back to working out, and his six-pack was looking better than ever.

Brandon gleamed at his complexion in Lynn's bedroom mirror. *You handsome muthafucka, you.* He popped the collar to his shirt, flashed his pearly white teeth, and proceeded out into the living room behind Lynn.

When he got to the bedroom door, he heard a squeaking noise coming from across the room. He stepped back into the room and headed over to see where it was coming from. He listened closely and determined that it must be coming from the bedroom closet. *I really hope she doesn't have mice.* Brandon grasped the doorknob to the closet and turned it slightly to the right.

"What are you doing?"

"Nothing. I thought I heard something coming from your closet." He let go of the knob and joined her across the room.

Mia's heart continued to pump fast as they left the room and walked out of the apartment. She flung the closet door open and gathered the rest of her clothing, which Lynn had kicked under the bed when Brandon came into the room. She put on her heels and wisped her hair out of her face and behind her ear. She put on her sunglasses and paced the living room floor, killing a little time, until she felt the coast was clear.

Mia couldn't understand for the life of her what Brandon saw in such a poorly dressed tart as Lynn. Yes, she had a nice personality and one hell of a curvaceous body, but she wasn't wifey material.

She hurried home from Lynn's apartment and picked up the baby from her play group. Brandon thought she was at a doctor's visit with the baby, so Mia swung by the pediatrician's office to show her face just in case he called and made her way home. As she maneuvered through Center City pushing the baby stroller, all she could see was Brandon's face light up when he saw Lynn. She knew that look. It was the same one he gave her when they'd first met.

Mia lay the baby down in her crib for her afternoon nap and plopped down on the couch to watch TV until Brandon got back home.


When they arrived at Bridget Foy's restaurant on South Street, it was more crowded than usual. Their usual cozy table by the bay window in the back had been taken by an older white couple, so they were seated near the kitchen, one of the worst locations in the restaurant.

Lynn unfolded her napkin and placed it in her lap. She looked over at Brandon, who just happened to be staring at her at the time. "What are you looking at?" she asked, blushing from ear to ear.

"You, silly." Brandon grabbed her hand from across the table and kissed it. "You're just so beautiful. I could stare at you all day."

"Hello. My name is William, and I will be your server today." The tall brown-skinned man placed menus in front of both Brandon and Lynn.

Brandon, still staring at Lynn from across the table, quickly remembered that voice, well-spoken, conservative, and demanding attention. Just like the voice of Mia's father. He could tell that snobbish tone anywhere. He looked up at his salt-and-pepper beard and confirmed that it was indeed him. "What are you doing here, Mr. Woods?"

He smiled. "Sir, who is Mr. Woods? I just told you my name is William. Would you care to order a beverage?"

"Why would you be working here? Don't you own a real estate firm?"

Lynn stood by looking totally confused about the entire incident. She remained silent and continued listening to the conversation.

William shook his head. "I'm sorry, sir. You must have me mixed up with someone else. Now, would you like to order a beverage?"

Lynn tried to ease the confusion. "I'll have a glass of Chardonnay."

"Excuse me. Do you really not know who I am?"

"Sir, I have never seen you in my life." William was getting a little upset at this point.

"You're my wife's father. Here, look at the picture." Brandon pulled a wallet-sized photo out of his wallet of the wedding party and handed it to him.

Lynn tried to lean in and get a look of the picture, but it was too far away for her to get a good look.

William held the picture out to get a better look at it and then smiled. "Ohhhh, I remember this picture. This was from that acting gig I did last year. That sure was a beautiful wedding."

Brandon raised his voice. "Acting gig? What acting gig?"

"The young lady paid me and another actor to act like her parents. She said it was for press purposes." William handed the picture back to Brandon.

"Come to think of it, you do look familiar. I gave you a hard time, didn't I?" He let out a soft chuckle. "Now, are you ready to order?"

Brandon looked over at Lynn. "Give us a minute."

"No problem, sir."

Once he was away from the table, Brandon leaned over at Lynn and gave her a fake smile. "I'm sorry you had to see that. Listen, can we cancel lunch? I have a little running around to do."

"Sure. No problem." Lynn grabbed her purse and got up from her chair.

"I'll have them call you a cab out front. I'm sorry, baby." Brandon kissed her on the cheek. "I gotta go."

Brandon left out the restaurant like a bolt of lightning. He hailed a cab and made his way home to confront Mia.

As he took the short ride to his house, several thoughts raced through his mind. Who did he really marry? Was she really as wealthy as he made her out to be? Or was she really a fake like Chris said? If he confronted her, he knew she would just lie.

He knew exactly what he was going to do. He was going to go back to that restaurant and ask William to come to his house for dinner, just a little gesture of thanks for being part of their wedding. "Can you please turn back around and take me back to the restaurant?"

"Sure thing."

As the cab driver made a U-turn and headed back in the direction from which they'd just come, Brandon sat back comfortably and stared out of the window. Things weren't adding up, and he was going to find out the truth about Mia, or die trying.

Lynn waited in the vestibule of the restaurant for a cab. She was so annoyed that Brandon canceled their lunch date, but she refused to let it show. She decided to call Nina to see if she wanted to meet up.

"Hey, girl." Mia yawned into the phone. While waiting for Brandon to come back from his little lunch date, she'd fallen asleep on the couch.

"Hey, Nina. You feel like meeting up? My lunch date got canceled."

"Canceled? How did that happen?" Mia sat up from the couch.

"Some crazy stuff went on with the waiter. He claimed that the waiter was his wife's father and the man said he was just an actor."

"What restaurant were you at?"

"Bridget Foy's on South Street."

"Listen, let me get myself together, and I'll give you a call back."

Lynn saw a cab pulling up in front of the restaurant. "Call me at home."

"Okay, I'll talk to you in a little bit."

Mia hung up the phone and began scrambling around the house, trying to find a phone book. She looked in the cabinets under the kitchen sink and there they were. She grabbed one and flipped through to the restaurant section. She found the number to Bridget Foy's and dialed as fast as her little fingers would allow her.

"Hello," a woman answered.

"Yes. May I speak with William?" Mia put on her most snobbish voice.

"Sure, ma'am. Could you hold on for a minute?"

Mia took a seat on the stool at the kitchen counter and waited for him to answer.

"Hello."

"Hi, William. This is Mia, I don't know if you remember me, but you did an acting gig for me some time ago."

"Ahhh, young lady, I do remember. As a matter of fact, your husband just left here. How are you?"

"I'm doing well."

"That's good to hear." William was wondering when she was going to get to the point.

"Listen, William, I need you to do me a favor. My husband wasn't supposed to find out about you. I need you to quit that job of yours. I know he's going to come back there looking for you."

"Quit my job? I can't do that. I have a family to feed."

"What are they paying you there anyway?"

"About six hundred dollars a week?"

"I'll double that. I will meet you tomorrow at Love Park with the check, but I need you to quit *now*."

"Are you sure you'll be able to meet tomorrow? My rent is due."

"Look, like I said, meet me at Love Park at one p.m. tomorrow, and I'll have your money."

"I'll see you then." William placed the phone back into the hands of the hostess. Then he took off his apron and placed it in the hands of his boss, who just happened to be walking by.

The manager held up the apron as if it was infected. "What's this?"

"It's my apron. I'm done here."

"But you're in the middle of your shift." The manager continued holding the apron up in the air.

"I know." William smiled as he walked toward the front door and left the restaurant.


Lynn opened the window in the back of the cab and allowed the summer breeze to gently smack her in the face. Being with Nina was the most exciting sexual experience she'd ever had in her life, but Brandon was her soul mate. When she was around him, she felt at ease, and it just felt right. She had no idea that her relationship with Nina would become so deep.

She had a choice to make, and fast. Almost getting caught in her apartment with another woman by Brandon was something she never wanted to experience again. She didn't want to lose either one of them, and she didn't want to play with their feelings either.

Nina was a single woman who reminded her of a female version of Brandon. She enjoyed the finer things in life and always treated her like a queen. Brandon, on the other hand, was still married. Lynn knew it sounded crazy, but she wasn't ready to give up on him just yet. She knew that the more time they spent together, the more he would realize he'd made a big mistake by letting her go. Lynn decided she was going to have to let Nina know that their relationship could no longer include sex. It had to be platonic, or nothing at all.

Brandon bypassed the reservation desk and stormed into the dining hall area of the restaurant in search of William. He searched the entire area and after scanning the room several times to see if he would pop up, decided to ask one of the kitchen staff who was walking past.

"Excuse me, sir." Brandon cleared his throat. "I'm looking for William. He's a waiter here."

"Willy just quit." The young Mexican man headed toward the kitchen

Brandon followed him through the swinging doors. "What do you mean, he just quit?"

"He said he came into some money, and he quit. He handed the manager his apron and walked out."

Brandon shook his head in disbelief. Just when he thought he had concrete proof that Mia was up to something, it fell through. He walked out of the restaurant and onto South Street. He walked up the street, and then it hit him. He needed to get home as fast as he could to check that jewelry box for that pendant. Brandon stood on the corner of 3rd and South Streets and hailed a cab. He jumped in and demanded that the cabbie took him to his apartment building as fast as he could.

When Brandon arrived back at the apartment building, the first thing he did was stop in the lobby to see if Nate, the weekend doorman, was still around. He saw him off to the side, by the elevators, cleaning out ashtrays.

"Hey, Nate. Can I talk to you for a moment?" Brandon looked around the lobby.

"Sure, Mr. B." Nate stopped in the middle of his cleaning. "What's up?"

"Remember that lady that was in here earlier?" Brandon asked, keeping his voice down.

"Yes, of course," Nate said, lowering his voice also.

"Have you seen her in here before?"

"Once before, but that was a while back."

"Could you do me a favor? If you happen to see her again, could you let me know?"

"I sure can."

Brandon handed Nate a crisp fifty-dollar bill, stepped on the elevator, and waited for the doors to close. His second mission was to check Mia's jewelry box for the pendant he'd bought her for Valentine's Day.

Mia was in the nursery with the baby when he arrived, changing her pamper. Brandon peeked in briefly and then headed across to the bedroom. Sitting down at her vanity table, Brandon's eyes looked over the countless beauty products aligned neatly across her table.

He then came across Mia's handcrafted wooden jewelry box. He opened it carefully, making sure to not make a peep, and searched through it, going through each piece one by one. The pendant wasn't there.

Brandon closed the jewelry box. *There must be a logical reason as to why the pendant is gone. There is no way in hell Mia would know how to find Lynn.*

He got up from the vanity table and sat on the side of the bed. He had more investigating to do, and in order to get it done, he needed to get rid of Mia for an entire day. He knew exactly how to get her out of the house. It was too late to set it up for today, but tomorrow could definitely work in his favor.

Brandon sifted through his wallet for the card to the day spa and called ahead and made her an appointment for early tomorrow morning.


Mia put the baby in her swing and joined Brandon in the bedroom. She sat down at her vanity table and brushed her hair. Her story was already planned out if Brandon asked her about William. She was going to say that it was her father's twin brother. Far-fetched, she knew, but she just needed to buy at least a month's worth of time to finish her plans up.

Mia instantly knew that Brandon had been through her things. She kept her jewelry box on an angle, and it was put back in a straight position. She sat quietly as if everything was fine and began moisturizing her face with Crème de la Mer moisturizing cream.

Brandon looked over at her as she began to hum lightly. Biting his tongue was taking too much out of him. He said casually, "Hey, baby. Where's that pendant I got you for Valentine's Day?"

"It's at the jeweler being cleaned, along with my wedding rings." Mia wiggled her fingers in front of him, to reveal her bare ring finger.

Mia smiled at herself in the mirror. She loved manipulating Brandon. After all the bullshit he put her through, it finally made her feel good to see him squirm. He knew something was up, but he was too stupid to figure it out. And by the time he did, it would be too late.

Brandon remained silent. He had to admit, she was good at what she did. He just had to be better.

He got up from the bed, undressed, and placed a towel

around his thick waist. He then went into the bathroom to take a shower. He needed time away from her to think, and what better place than the bathroom.

Brandon dried off and made his way to the kitchen for a cold Heineken. He popped the top and took several long gulps. He then placed the half-empty bottle on the counter and made his way to the nursery to check on Kai, who was sound asleep. He then went across to the bedroom where Mia was lying in bed watching TV and talking on the phone.

He slid into the bed next to and cuddled up on her chest to eavesdrop on her conversation. He could hear a woman's voice on the other side of the phone, but he couldn't make out exactly what was being said.

Mia pushed him to the side and eased herself from up under him. She smiled warmly as she got up from the bed and made her way to the bathroom, the receiver still glued to the side of her head. She sat on the toilet to finish up her conversation.

Brandon slid out of bed behind her and silently moved across the room to peep through the slightly cracked door. He listened carefully as she whispered into the phone and laughed faintly.

"I miss you too, sweetie." She purred crossing her legs as if the person on the other end could see her.

"I can't wait to see you either. I miss those soft lips of yours caressing my kitty."

Brandon stood by in shock and anger. His body shook uncontrollably as he imagined another man sexing his wife. He backed away from the door and lay back down in the bed. *How could she? The no-good whore.*

Brandon tried to recount other times where she may have

lied to him and he believed her, and realized there were too many to remember. He felt like getting up and choking her to death.

He watched her every move as she made her way around the bed and slid in beside him. She placed the receiver on the hook and then snuggled up next to him.

Brandon turned his back to her and acted as if he was trying to get comfortable. "I booked you a day at the spa."

"Thanks, babe."

Mia wrapped her arms around his solid body. She leaned over him and tried to give him a kiss on the lips, but he pulled away. She didn't say a word. She just turned her back to him also, smiling to herself. She knew he'd heard every word of her conversation while she was in the bathroom, just like she intended him to. *He is such a gullible asshole.* She buried her head into her pillow and closed her eyes.

Now that she had an appointment at the spa, she had an excuse to get out of the house to pay William and finish up a couple other errands important to her plan. In thirty days, she would be living off the shores of Belize, sipping on cocktails and basking in the sun.

It was never her intention to hurt Brandon, but after he seeing him with that physical therapist at the hospital, she just snapped. After all she'd done for him, she would never be enough. So if he couldn't be with just her, he couldn't be with anybody.

Brandon gritted his teeth as he tried to control himself. He felt like grabbing Mia's head and smashing it through the headboard of their bed. That phone call confirmed everything Chris had said about her. There was no doubt about it—She was a whore.

Knowing that he married the wrong woman made Brandon's stomach sour. Lynn was the woman for him; he just didn't know how to go about pursuing her, seeing he had a wife and a child.

Divorcing Mia wasn't such a bad idea, but that meant a custody battle, and of course, a huge alimony payment that was sure to keep him in the poor house.

# Chapter 12

### Judgment Day, Part 1
### Chris

"Come to Atlanta with me," Chris begged, squeezing Tracy's hand tight and looking deep into her eyes, as if he could see her soul.

"I-I-I don't know."

Tracy remembered Hakeem's threat. She was risking her life just by meeting up with Chris on a weekly basis. In her mind, it was a risk well worth taking. Chris was the father of her child, and she would've liked nothing more than to go back to the way things used to be. Knowing that Chris was bi-sexual was a hard pill to swallow, but his being in her life made her somehow feel complete.

"Come on, baby, I got enough saved up for us to get a crib. It'll be nice. Nobody will know us. We can start over."

Chris's offer was quite enticing. Hakeem couldn't possibly find her in Atlanta. She bit her bottom lip. "Just us, huh."

"Just us." Chris planted a big wet kiss on her cheek, causing her to blush wildly.

"Can I think about it?"

"Come, baby. How long you need to think about it? Me, you, and the baby—That's all we need."

Tracy squeezed his hand back. "Give me a week."

Chris sighed. "A week it is."

Tracy looked up at the clock over the mantelpiece in Ms.

Ruth's house. It was nearly four p.m. Hakeem would be home in a few short hours, expecting dinner to be served as soon as he sat down to the table. She left Chris's warm embrace and gathered Li'l Chris from the floor and placed him on her hip. She gave Chris a good-bye kiss and headed for the front door.

Chris walked behind her and Li'l Chris and waited for them to safely back out the driveway. He watched as they drove down the street and made a left at the corner. He closed the door and went back in the house. He began cleaning up Li'l Chris's toys and placing them back in the toy chest.

Chris was so close to having his family back, there was no way he was going to let anybody come in between him and Tracy again. She didn't know about De'Andre, and he wanted to make sure it stayed that way. Instead of breaking it off with him and have to worry about him destroying his family, he figured moving out of the state with no knowledge of his whereabouts was a surefire plan. All he had to do was get fifty grand more, and he would be straight. That would be enough for them to live comfortably for at least three years.

Chris finished cleaning up the toys and turned out all the lights in the house. He then locked the door and made his way to his car. He blew his breath into the cold winter air and inhaled what he knew was going to be a new life. There was no way Tracy could tell him no. He knew she was tired of Hakeem whipping her ass every other day. He sure was.

Chris had promised he would stay out of it, and so far he had. He was just tired of seeing the hurt in her eyes every time he'd see her with a black eye or busted lip.


Chris made his way back to the boarding house where he shared a room with Shawn. He hadn't been staying there much lately, but to keep things cool until he moved to Atlanta, he made daily appearances there to satisfy Shawn.

When he walked through the door, Shawn was sitting on the edge of the bed, talking on his cell phone. As soon as he saw Chris standing in front of him, he flipped the phone closed and placed it in his pocket.

"I didn't hear you come in. So where you coming from?"

"My mom's crib. I still had a couple of things to clean out of the house before they put it on the market."

Chris went over to the closet and grabbed the Nike duffel bag he used to pick up the week's work from his team out in the streets.

"I'll be back in a little bit. I gotta go handle some business."

"But you just got here," Shawn said, yawning as he talked.

"Look, I gotta go make this money. So I'll see you later."

"De'Andre came by here looking for you."

Chris stopped at the front door of their tiny room. "Oh yeah? What he want?"

"He said he had some news that might be of interest to you. He said you knew how to get with him."

Chris nodded his head and continued out the door and down the steps. De'Andre didn't know where he lived, so he found it hard to believe. Especially after the ass-whupping he'd given him a few months back.

When Chris reached his car, De'Andre was leaning against the driver's side door, his hands in his pockets, and wearing a pair of sunglasses so dark, Chris was unable to see his eyes.

"What you want, man?" Chris folded his hands in front of his chest.

"I need to talk to you about some business." De'Andre took off his sunglasses and held them in his hand. "Take a walk with me."

"Look, man, I ain't got time for this dumb shit. What the fuck you want?"

"Never mind, nigga," De'Andre said, placing his glasses

back on his face. "Since you want to act like that, I'll let you find out the hard way. Just remember, Chief, you made your own grave." He pulled his hood on his head and walked off.

Chris got in the car and drove off. He shook his head. *That nigga talking shit. Don't know what the hell he's talking about.*

He stopped at each of his corners and collected his money for the week. He gave each worker a new batch of work, even though he knew wouldn't be around to collect from it. He didn't care what happened to the profit, as long as he was able to make a clean break without anyone noticing.

When he arrived back at the boarding house, it was one a.m. in the morning. Shawn was snoring so loud, Chris could hear him from the hallway. He took his shoes off at the door and eased himself inside, making sure not to make any noise. The last thing he wanted to hear was Shawn's mouth.

He undressed and got into the bed beside him. He noticed Shawn's cell phone on the bed beside him, lighting up with a new message. He picked it up and flipped it open to see who was calling him so late at night. He scrolled through the log, and saw a missed call from De'Andre.

Chris threw the phone back on the bed and closed his eyes. He didn't know what Shawn was up to, and he really didn't care. In a couple of days, he would be in Atlanta with his family, and Shawn would be free to do whatever his heart desired.


Tracy squirmed under Hakeem's 250-pound frame. "You're hurting me!"

"Stay still then!" he yelled, pushing all of his weight into her.

Hakeem's eyes darkened as he reached down between her legs and pushed his two fingers into her pussy. His breath reeked of Colt 45 malt liquor. He kissed savagely at her neck and face, biting down on her skin.

"Please, Hakeem, I think I hear the baby in the other room. I need to go check on him."

Hakeem just dug deeper into her flesh. He began fidgeting with his belt until he got it loose. "You're gonna shut the fuck up and take this dick. That's what you're gonna do."

"But I need to—"

*Wham!* Hakeem's palm slammed across her face.

He pulled out his swollen dick and stroked it. He grabbed both of her thighs tightly, forced them open, and planted himself between them again. He rubbed his dick against her pussy to get her wet, but it just wasn't working.

"So you don't want my dick, huh?" He moved from in between her legs and rested his dick on her lips. "Suck it!" He grabbed her jaw and forced her mouth open.

Tracy closed her eyes and planted her mouth on his swollen member, and he guided her head as she slobbered all over him. To Tracy's delight, once his dick was nice and moistened, he backed off her and began stroking himself lightly.

"Turn over." He was still holding his manhood in his hand and looking at her naked body as if she was a piece of meat.

Without arguing, Tracy did as instructed. He'd relieved himself plenty times on her back when he masturbated, so she just hoped he would hurry and get it over with.

Hakeem continued to stroke himself as he towered over Tracy's round bubble. He palmed her left check as he continued to get himself off. Almost at his peak, he decided to try something different. He spread her cheeks apart, licked his right index finger, and plunged into her asshole, causing her to buck.

Tracy lifted her head from the pillow. "What are you doing?"

He pushed her head back down into the pillow and pulled his finger out, replacing it with the tip of his swollen rod.

Just as he was just about in, Li'l Chris appeared at the bedroom door and began screaming.

Hakeem turned around and approached Li'l Chris. "Go back to your room!" he yelled at the top of his lungs, pointing in the direction of his room.

Li'l Chris stood still and continued to whine.

Hakeem raised his hand and Tracy rushed over and grabbed Li'l Chris shielding him with her naked body. Hakeem pushed her aside causing her to hit her head on the wall and pushed Li'l Chris into the hallway and locked the bedroom door. He then pulled Tracy to her feet and pressed her naked body against the wall and forced himself into her from behind. The tightness of her ass as he gyrated in and out of her made his entire body quiver.

"You're gonna give me what's mine." He said pulling her hair with his right hand as his continued to pen her up against the wall. After five more strokes, Hakeem pulled out, pushed Tracy to her knees, and relieved himself on her lips. He then took his hand and smeared his cum all over her face.

Tracy leaned against the wall and pressed her knees against the rest of her petite frame. She rocked back and forth as the excruciating pain took over her body. She could hear Li'l Chris whimpering on the other side of the door, but she was too scared to move, not knowing what Hakeem might do to her next. She watched as he climbed into bed, a look of satisfaction on his face, and turned on the television.

"Go make me a sandwich, I'm hungry."

Tracy picked herself up from the bedroom floor and put on her robe that hung on the closet door. When she exited the bedroom to the hallway, Li'l Chris was huddled up in a ball at the end of the hallway. She picked him up from the floor, carried him to his room, and placed him back in his bed. She then went down to the kitchen and made Hakeem a sandwich.

When she got back upstairs, he was laying on his back, snoring, with the TV watching him. She placed the saucer with the sandwich beside him on the night table and eased into bed next to him. She turned her back away from him and cried herself to sleep as she did every night.


Chris waited anxiously by the front window that overlooked the porch at his mother's house. It was Thursday again, and he and Tracy planned to meet at noon as they did every week on that day. Today was special for him because he was going to find out if Tracy was going away with him. He was prepared to leave as early as Saturday night if she said yes. He didn't plan to take much, just the clothes on his back and the duffel bag full of money he had stashed in the closet behind the wall panel upstairs in his room.

Tracy pulled into the driveway and turned the car off. She looked at her jaw in the rearview mirror. The swelling had gone down some; it didn't look as bad as she thought. She applied a coat of Chap Stick to her lips and got out the car to unstrap Li'l Chris from his car seat. She then led him up the stairs and to the house.

Chris met her at the door and gave her a long welcoming kiss. He noticed her jaw was swollen but didn't say anything. She'd told him on more than one occasion that she could handle her own business, so he had to just trust that she would do so. He grabbed Li'l Chris up into his arms and hugged him tight. He then sat down with him on his lap and waited silently for her answer.

Tracy paced back in forth in the living room. She wasn't sure if she was making the right choice, but she did know that Hakeem was getting more violent and she needed to get out of there. "When do we leave?" she asked, a weak smile on her face.

Chris sensed her uneasiness. "Are you sure?"

"Chris, I just don't want to have to worry about you cheating on me again. My heart can't take that."

Ms. Ruth's death made him come to grips with some of the most painful times in his life. After doing a lot of soul-searching, he realized that his craving for men was merely a coverup for the guilt he felt as a child while being molested.

Grabbing her hand in his, he said, "I promise you, on everything I love, that I will never cheat on you again. I messed up once, and I promised myself that if I ever got a second chance, there would be nobody or no thing that could come between me and my family. Do you trust me?"

"Yes, I trust you." Tracy joined him on the sofa. "So when do we leave?"

"Saturday night. I just have to tie up some loose ends. Meet me down at the stables around eleven, and don't bring anything but you and Li'l Chris. We'll buy whatever we need when we get down there."

Tracy was excited about moving to a place where no one knew who she was.

Chris put the baby in the middle of them and leaned over to kiss Tracy. He caressed her back as their tongues intertwined. Li'l Chris took his little arms and pried them apart, as they were beginning to squeeze him. They both laughed as he folded his arms across his little chest and began to pout.

Tracy took him into his lap, Chris took her into his arms, and they all sat silently on the couch as one happy family, just as both Chris and Tracy imagined.

When Chris drove up the dirt road to the old horse stables, Tracy was yet to arrive. Nervous, his mind began racing. *What if she changed her mind? Or, even worse, what if she really did love that nut-ass nigga Hakeem?*

Chris took several deep breaths in a row and tried to relax. They'd been texting each other all week about how excited they were. He continued to watch the time. It was now ten after eleven and still no sign of her. Just as he was about to lose hope, Tracy came roaring through the parking lot.

Tracy jumped out of the car and unstrapped Li'l Chris from his car seat. "I'm so sorry, I'm late." She led him over to Chris's car and strapped him in the car seat Chris had in place. She then gave Chris a big hug and kiss. "I know you thought I wasn't coming."

"Yeah. You had me scared for a minute there," Chris said, holding her by the waist.

Tracy blushed. "I love you, Chris, and I always have. Now let's get out of here." She left his warm embrace and made her way over to the passenger side of the car and got in.

Just as Chris was about to get in the car, Hakeem sped up in a black tinted-out Expedition. He jumped out with his gun drawn and waved it at Chris for him to step away from the car.

As Chris moved closer in his direction, he realized who it was. His lips perched in anger. "What the fuck are you doing here?" He looked around the parking lot to see if there was anyone else around. "Why don't you stop trying to be a hero and take your nut ass home? She don't want you."

"She wants whatever I tell her to. Besides, nigga, this ain't about her, this about you and me, and my brother."

"Who's your brother, nigga?" Chris wasn't shaken by Hakeem's threat. He slowly positioned his hand under his shirt to get to the pistol lodged in the waist of his jeans.

"You killed my brother, and now it's your turn to die."

"Get the fuck out of here! Ain't nobody kill ya brother." Chris flagged him and turned to walk away.

"Mike was my brother, nigga! And you killed him!"

The only source of lighting in the entire parking lot, a dim street lamp, now trickled down on Hakeem's face, which was filled with hatred.

Mike was a rival of Chris's from the projects that he had rocked some time ago. He'd tried to kill Chris, but like Tank, was unsuccessful.

Chris's memory reverted back to seeing him with Mike a few times. As he looked closer, he thought they did resemble each other. Chris always kept telling himself he knew him from somewhere but just couldn't place him.

Noticing Chris's arm moving toward his waist, Hakeem let off two shots to his chest, causing Chris's body to jerk backwards as the bullets tore though his body.

"Now what, nigga?" Hakeem cocked the gun back and aimed it at Chris's chest. He chuckled wildly. "I had your bitch and your kid, and now I got you. You stupid nigga! I even paid De'Andre to warn you because I knew you were too dumb to listen to him."

Chris's body fell to the ground in what seemed like slow motion.

Hakeem stood over him and let off three more shots, hitting him in the abdomen. He then looked over at Tracy, who was screaming as she held on to Li'l Chris.

"Let's see what this nigga can do for you now. I'm done with you, bitch. I never wanted you in the first place. I just wanted that dumb-ass nigga to know how easy it was to get to him." He placed his gun back in its holster. He walked calmly back to his car, got in, and sped off without looking back.

Chris closed his eyes and accepted his fate. The burning shot through his body like lightning, and he could feel his body starting to shut down.

His life flashed before his eyes—his mother, his friendship with Brandon, Tracy, Li'l Chris. And every bad deed he'd done to anyone.

Chris never thought his life would end up like this. He knew there were consequences to being a hustler and living a life of crime, but for a moment there, he felt invincible. I guess it was like his mother said, "On your day of judgment, you will be held accountable for your sins."

One of his biggest regrets was missing out on being the family man he so desperately wanted to be, because of the life he lived

As Chris drifted in and out of consciousness, he managed to whisper to Tracy, who was now sobbing by his side, "Take my car and get out of here. Go to Atlanta," he said, fighting through short gasps of air. "Everything you'll need is in the trunk. Hurry up before the cops come. I love you, babe." Blood began to seep out of the crack of his mouth, and his body jerked around in spasms and then went limp on the cold sidewalk.

Tracy fought through her tears as she hurried back to Chris's car like he instructed. She turned out of the dirt parking lot heading toward 95 South. She could hear the sirens roaring down from a few blocks over.

*How could I have been so stupid?*

When she met Hakeem, she'd never imagined he would have turned out to be such a monster. He was so nice to Tracy and Li'l Chris.

*All of this just to get to Chris?*

Her mind flashed to the last time she'd seen him smile; it was only minutes ago when she'd pulled up into the parking lot. A look of relief glazed over his face when he realized that she didn't change her mind.

She kept telling him that the life he lived was going to come back to bite him in the ass. She just never thought it would happen like this.

Tracy wiped at her tears as she looked in the back seat at Li'l

Chris, who was sound asleep in his car seat. She flew down Girard Avenue until she reached the expressway. "This is it," she said out loud, trying to convince herself that everything was going to be all right. "This is the start of my new life."

# Chapter 13

### Judgment Day, Part 2
### Brandon

Brandon stretched his arms out and yawned loudly. He looked over his right shoulder, only to see an empty space beside him. He then looked over at the clock. It was barely eight a.m., and she was already out of the house. He sat up on the side of the bed and slipped on his leather bed shoes. He then got up from the bed and headed to the nursery to check on Kai. When he got to the door of the nursery, he noticed she too was gone. *Mia must have taken her to her play group.*

Brandon leaned against the kitchen counter as he sipped on a cup of freshly brewed coffee. He noticed a pile of mail sitting in the middle of the counter with his name on it, so he decided to sit down and open it up as he continued his morning cup of java.

Brandon had just recently started drinking coffee after starting to play detective, trying to find out what Mia was up to, and it was definitely taking a toll on his body. His efforts weren't in vain, though. With the help of Nate, he was able to find out where the mysterious woman who kept coming to their apartment building stayed. He was told that she spent most of her nights in a women's shelter, so he checked every night in hopes that he would find her. He hadn't run into her yet, but he knew it was only a matter of time before they crossed paths.

Brandon opened the drawer next to the refrigerator and returned to the counter with Tiffany's letter opener one of Mia's so-called family members had given them as a wedding gift. He then took a seat back at the counter and opened up the first of four letters addressed to him. The first one was from Hartford Insurance Company, where Mia and he held all their policies. He slid the opener across the sealed envelope and removed the letter. He took another sip of his coffee and began reading. It was a letter from customer service, asking if he was satisfied with the recent changes to his life insurance premium. Brandon pushed away from the counter in confusion and quickly grabbed the phone to dial the 1-800 number to speak with a representative.

"Hartford Insurance," a cheery feminine voice answered.

"Hello there," Brandon said in the most distinguished voice he could muster. "I'm trying to get some information on my policy. Would you be able to help me with that?"

"Sure, sir. May I have your account information?"

Brandon gave her the account information and waited for her to pull up the account.

"Mr. Brandon Brunson?"

"Yes, that's me."

"What can I do for you, Mr. Brunson?"

"There were some recent changes made to my life insurance policy, and I was wondering what exactly those changes entailed."

"Well, Mr. Brunson, it looks as though your wife upped your benefit by five hundred thousand dollars, which would now make you insured up to one million. Of course, your premium went up too."

"I didn't sign off on those changes."

"I'm afraid you didn't have to, Mr. Brunson. Either one of you can make changes to the account at any time."

Without saying another word, Brandon slammed the phone down on the cradle and pounded the counter with his fist. He threw the letter to the side and continued going through the stack of mail. He finally got down to the last piece of mail, a brown envelope marked "Confidential." He looked it over and opened it with his bare hands, ripping the paper slightly in the process. He thought it was one of those Publishers Clearing House attempts to make him think he won some money.

Brandon quickly searched the envelope and found a check inside for $250,000. After carefully reviewing the letter, he learned that it was from Ms. Ruth's estate. Tears trickled down his face as he thought of how much he missed both Ms. Ruth and his mother.

Brandon kissed his newfound wealth and headed to the bedroom to throw on some clothes, so he could go to the bank before Mia came home. He was going to open up a new account and place the check inside for safekeeping. If Mia found out about the money, she would try to spend every dime of it until it was gone. He only had $7,000 left in his account that she knew of, and he planned to keep it that way.

After Brandon left the bank, he decided to pass by the women's shelter to see if could find the woman he had been looking for. He had made friends with one of the staffmembers, who was able to sneak him into the side door every time he went to search for her. Men weren't allowed in the shelter unless they worked there, so Brandon had to make sure he looked as if he was a social worker. He'd made sure to put on a pair of stain-proof Dockers, a navy blue Polo collared shirt and some brown Oxfords, and to top it off, a pair of wire-rimmed glasses that wasn't prescribed.

Brandon arrived at the back door of the shelter just in time to catch the women at lunch. He walked through the cafeteria, making sure to take in every face that sat at the picnic-style tables. After his second time around, he noticed the light-skinned woman sitting in a corner by herself hovered over her tomato soup and grilled cheese sandwich.

He pulled up a chair beside her and smiled warmly. "Hi there," he said, settling down in his seat.

"Hi," she said without looking up. She seemed too busy to make conversation for fear of missing out on her meal.

Brandon lowered his voice so no one else in the crowded cafeteria could hear. "Can I talk to you for a minute?"

She looked up from her plate and dropped the other half of her grilled cheese sandwich back down on it. She took the napkin from the side of her plate and wiped tomato soup from her mouth. She looked at Brandon once more. "How did you find me? And who told you to come here?"

"You know my wife, don't you?"

Her eyes glistened with fear at the thought of Mia finding out that he'd been here to visit her. "No. I don't know her. I mean, I don't know her like that."

Brandon didn't have time to play these types of games. He pulled a crisp hundred-dollar bill out of his pocket and placed it on top of what was left of her grilled cheese sandwich. "Let's try this again—Do you know my wife?" Brandon asked, raising his voice just a little.

The woman grabbed the crisp bill of her plate. "Yeah, I know her."

"How do you know her?"

"Tifah's my daughter." The woman returned to her tomato soup.

"Tifah?" Brandon repeated, trying to grasp what the woman had just told him.

Brandon had met Mia's mother, and she looked nothing like the skinny, toothless woman beside him. He knew she had to be telling the truth. Mia had hired William, the waiter from the restaurant, to play her father, so he knew what she was capable of.

He looked closely at the woman's features. She had the same high cheekbones and the same big hazel eyes. Brandon knew that in her day, she was most likely a knockout. *Drugs will do that to you.* Brandon said as he continued to look her over. Her tattered jean shorts held holes in them up her thighs, and her once-white flip-flops were now a shade of dingy gray.

"So her real name is Tifah?"

"Latifah. She changed her name when she turned eighteen."

"Oh, okay. So where is her father?"

"He dead." She finished off her soup and placed the bowl back down on the table. "He OD'd 'bout five years ago. Tifah ain't never wanted none of us coming 'round her. She said we embarrass her."

"Now, why would she say a thing like that?" Brandon asked sarcastically.

"Don't know. She say we too ghetto for her. Tifah always thought she was better than her other sisters and brothers."

Brandon was at the edge of his seat now. "Sister and brothers? How many?"

"Five sisters and three brothers." She looked around the room. "If Tifah finds out I've been talking to you, she gonna be real mad, and when she get mad, she can be a trip."

"Tell me about it."

"No, you don't understand. The last time she got mad wit' me, she had me put in the nut house for six months. I kept telling them doctors there was nothing wrong with me, but she convinced them that I was a basket case. I might be a lot of things, but I ain't crazy."

"I understand," Brandon said, sympathizing with her.

Brandon's mind raced as he tried to figure out how he got caught up with such a horrible woman. He knew what it was. Her money. She was crazy, yes, but he'd rather be with someone crazy and rich than someone who was just flat-out broke.

"I just have one more question, and then I'll never bother you again."

"Hurry up. That girl got peoples watching everywhere. She told me that if she ever found out that I talked to you she would put me back in the nut house and make sure I never get out."

"So I take it that all the money she has came from her modeling career and not her family?"

The woman laughed. "Tifah ain't got no real money, chile. She uses men like you to fund her lifestyle."

"But, but, I seen her bank statements."

"She got you with them phony bank statements too, huh? She did the same thing to her first and second husbands."

"First and second husbands?" Brandon yelled out, forgetting where he was for a moment.

"Honey, I hope you didn't think you were the only one."

"Thanks for your info. I have to go." Brandon got up from the table and walked off.

Brandon slipped out of the back door just as fast as he slipped in and made his way back to the condo building. His mind went back to when he and Chris were in Ms. Ruth's hospital room. Chris had told him that Mia was a whore, but he didn't believe him. Brandon thought he was just jealous that he had scored a rich chick, while he was stuck fucking niggas in the ass.

Brandon finally got back to the building. He was relieved to see that Mia was still out with the baby. He kicked off his shoes at the front door and sat down on the couch with a cold

Heineken. He knew his relationship with Mia, or should he say Tifah, was coming to a close. Plus, his relationship with Lynn was heating up. He was going to promise that once he divorced Mia, he would marry her. In fact, he had plans on going to the lawyer's office tomorrow to have the papers drawn up. He just didn't have the energy to keep playing detective. He found out enough information to be granted a divorce with a hassle.

Just as he was about to turn on the TV, in came Mia with Kai in the stroller. She left the stroller in the middle of the living room with Kai still strapped inside and headed back to the bedroom. Shaking his head, he pulled the stroller over to him so he could take her out.

Mia walked straight back to the bedroom and peeled out of the peach Juicy Couture sweat suit, which was hugging her body in all the right places. She made her way to the bathroom and turned on the shower.

She'd had an eventful morning. While Brandon thought she had taken the baby to the playgroup, she was really putting the finishing touches on her plan. Her property in Mexico had finally come through. Her first stop was at the realtor's office to close on the villa she'd found by the ocean. She then went and cashed out Brandon's bank account, which only held a measly ten grand at this point, but she refused to leave anything behind. Her last stop was at Lynn's apartment. Ever since Lynn had given Mia a key over a month ago, Mia would spend over an hour preparing her apartment for the grand finale every day Lynn was at school.

Mia stepped into the shower and massaged Carol Daughter's Almond Cookie Sea Salt Body Scrub into her skin in circular motions.

Lynn, mesmerized by Mia's body, had fallen prey to her beautiful looks, just as Brandon did, and Mia took advantage of it, using her for some good girl-on-girl action, and of course, as part of her plan.

Mia almost felt sorry for Lynn; she was just so naive. When Mia was her age, she was already living in a mansion with her white lawyer friend out in Ardmore, PA. All Lynn had acquired was a small one-bedroom apartment in what used to be one of the most respected condo buildings in the city, because once they started renting out apartments to college students, it was downhill from there.

Mia finished up her shower and dried off. When she returned from the bathroom, Brandon was sitting on the side of the bed with some papers lying beside him, his hands folded and a look of concern on his face. She hoped he wasn't going to start one of his lectures about money, because she was in no mood for it. She sat down at her vanity table and applied her face cream.

"Where do you get off upping my insurance policy without telling me?"

"Honey, I mentioned it to you some time ago," Mia said sheepishly. "When I added Kai to our policy, I decided to up not only yours but mine also."

Brandon couldn't remember the conversation. It didn't matter anyway. *That's okay*, Brandon thought. He was done with her and her lies. After he filed those papers he was going to take his daughter and go stay with Lynn. He'd already discussed it with her.

He grabbed the papers off the bed, made his way to the kitchen, and grabbed a bottle of Seagram's Gin out of the cupboard. He opened it up and took a long swig straight from the bottle.

Spying on Mia wasn't the only thing Brandon was doing in his spare time. He'd also managed to find him a job at Philadelphia International, one of the leading recording labels in

Philadelphia, as the head of public relations, with a salary of 90k, and was going to start his new life on Monday—a new job, a new woman, and most of all, a new Brandon.

Over the past few months, Lynn had taught Brandon that he could indeed love just one woman, but the right woman. He couldn't stay faithful to Mia because she wasn't the woman for him. He used to think she was, but she had showed him in so many ways that she wasn't.

Lynn cared about his feelings and encouraged him to get back into the workforce. She made him realize that life with money and the wrong person meant nothing. He'd rather live a mediocre life with someone he knew would complete him than with a money-hungry socialite who only cared about herself.

Brandon wanted to kick himself in the ass for being stupid enough to marry Mia. It was the worst mistake of his life, and he regretted it every day. If it wasn't for her, he believed he and Chris might have still been friends. Brandon felt that he'd allowed his greed to make him do things to please her that he would have never done otherwise, betraying his best friend, his brother, for a hoe-ass wannabe glamor model in four-inch Manolo Blahniks.

He looked up at the clock on the kitchen wall as he took another swig from the bottle. It was going on one p.m., and he was due to meet Lynn at her house later on this evening. She'd said she had a surprise for him, and he couldn't wait to see what it was. Last time she told him that, she'd gotten her kitty waxed in the shape of a B. He put the gin back in the cupboard and headed for the nursery to check on the baby.

Mia continued applying her makeup without any care of what Brandon had to say about the insurance policy. It didn't matter; she had done what needed to be done in order to secure her future. She finished up by applying M•A•C Lustre

Glass to her lips and sprayed Chanel perfume on her wrists and rubbed them together. She then went over to her closet and pulled out a pair of black Paige boot-cut jeans paired with a peach Marc Jacobs funnel-neck top that complemented her skin tone.

She sat back down at her vanity and picked through her jewelry box for the prefect accessories, wanting to look just right for this perfect occasion. She placed 1-ct. diamond cut studs in her ears and smiled at her reflection. *I'm a self-made woman with nothing to lose*, she thought to herself, continuing to stare in the mirror. She grabbed her purse from the closet and her black Gucci wrap. She then placed her Chanel aviator glasses on her face and headed out the bedroom door.

She doubled back to grab the bag of clothes she'd set aside in a brown shopping bag and headed out. *That was close*, she thought. Leaving the clothes behind would've ruined her entire plan. "Be back," she said, leaving out the door without taking time to look in Brandon's direction.

Brandon turned around just in time enough to see the door close behind her. He went back to watching TV. He was actually glad to see her go. He was at the point he could care less what she did. He closed his eyes and envisioned Lynn's face in his mind. He smiled faintly, fantasizing about her soft kisses and her warm, tight pussy.


With her purse under one hand and the brown bag in the other, Mia hurried out the elevator and through the lobby, the pitter-patter of her Manolo's echoing throughout the corridor. She hailed a cab in front of the building and demanded that it take her a few blocks over to where Lynn lived.

She dug into her purse for the silver key. She smiled deviously as she examined the ridges like a locksmith. She'd managed to score a key from Lynn, who went out of town to visit her father, promising she would water her plants every other day while she was gone.

When she arrived at Lynn's apartment, she was nowhere in sight, just as Mia planned. Lynn was still in school, so there was plenty of time to set up before she got home. Mia was well aware that Lynn and Brandon were supposed to have dinner at her house today. In fact, she was the one that suggested that Lynn make him a home-cooked meal. That way, both of them would be in the apartment together.

She took off her coat, laid it on the couch, and traveled back to the bedroom and got to work. She put on a pair of red leather gloves and began taking out the clothes she'd packed neatly in the brown shopping bag. She emptied the second dresser drawer of Lynn's oak armoire, which contained her unmentionables, and dumped them on the floor for the time being. She then placed Brandon's clothes neatly inside, making sure to put a mix of underwear and clothing inside, as if he was staying with her from time to time. She then sat down on the bed and pulled out a pad of stationery and a fancy fountain pen from Lynn's nightstand drawer and began to write a suicide note, addressing it to Brandon.

*Dear Brandon,*

*How could you betray me like this? You told me that you were going to leave her and now you decide to change your mind? I can't believe you would hurt me like this. I love you so much, and if I can't have you then no one can, including your wife.*

*Lynn*

Mia made sure it was sweet, simple, giving the police Lynn's motives for killing Brandon. She then placed the letter on the left side of the bed where Brandon often lay when he was there.

See, Lynn messed up big time. She told Mia everything about her relationship with Brandon, from his favorite cologne right down to his favorite sexual positions. Often, Mia wanted to get up and punch her in the face.

She then folded the bag up, placed it under her arm, and made her way back to the living area. She gathered her coat from the sofa and headed for the door. Her work was done there for now. All she had to do was show up tonight and make the sparks fly. She took one last look around the tiny apartment, a wicked grin on her face, and left out the door.

Mia hurried down the narrow hallway to the elevators and waited patiently for it to arrive. When the doors opened, she ran right into Lynn.

"What are you doing here?" Lynn asked, wrestling with her shopping bags as Mia brushed past her to take her place on the crowded elevator.

"I just passed by to get the diamond earrings I let you borrow. I have an important date tonight, and I need to look my best."

"You sure you can't stay for a while?" Lynn asked as the doors started to close.

"Sorry, babe, I can't. I'm already late for my hair appointment."

Lynn watched as the doors to the elevator slid shut. She hunched her shoulders and shuffled down the hallway to her apartment. She could have gone for some company, but she wasn't upset at all that Mia couldn't stay. In fact, she really needed to get ready for her date with Brandon tonight.

She placed the four grocery bags from Whole Foods on the kitchen counter and began laying out the ingredients to begin preparing the meal for tonight.

She was indeed excited. Brandon and her relationship was stronger and ever, and she just knew he was going to ask her to marry him. Recently, he had been talking about divorcing his wife and coming to live with her. She was going to cook his favorite meal and give him another present that he had been begging her for.

She laid the 12-ounce steaks out on the counter and began seasoning them up. After she got them in the oven, she was going to get the bedroom set up for what she knew was going to be the best night of her life.

After making a tossed salad and getting the meat in the oven, Lynn grabbed the last bag from the counter, which was full of sensual oils, incense, and candles, and headed toward the bedroom. She began placing the jasmine-scented pillar candles all over the bedroom, from the dresser tops to the windowsills. She then carefully placed the body oil and the incense in the holders beside the bed on the nightstand table.

Lynn's real surprise lay in the back of her closet. She went over to dig through the piles of clothes thrown at the bottom until she came across the box that held her video camera. After digging behind a few old textbooks, she finally came across the little JVC Micro Cam her father had bought her for Christmas a few years back. It was still in its original packaging because she really had no need to use it. Tonight she was going to give Brandon the time of his life, and put it on tape so he could watch over and over again.

He'd been begging her for months to do it; she just didn't have the heart until now. Lynn was a very sexual woman, but she kept it under wraps. Making a sex tape with the man she loved somehow intrigued her. Now that he was going to separate from his wife, there was no reason to hold back. They were celebrating him having the divorce papers drawn up and delivered to her. As of tomorrow, he would be free of his low-down, conniving wife she so easily came to hate hearing about. Although she'd never met her, from the way that Brandon described her she could tell that she was an opportunistic bitch who wanted him for his money.

Since he was willing to leave his wife for her, Lynn had no choice but to leave Nina alone at this point. Even though she enjoyed the sexual experience, she knew it had to come to an end sooner or later. She liked Nina a lot, and even felt herself falling for her from time to time, but she would give up the world to be with Brandon.

Nina was the perfect woman, and any man or woman she decided to deal with would indeed be a lucky person. She had the perfect body. Lynn shivered at the thought of touching Nina in between her thighs as she had done on so many occasions. Tasting Nina's sweetness was a treat for her. It was always so juicy. And Lynn loved the way Nina would run her hands through Lynn's thick reddish-brown Afro.

Besides that, she treated Lynn like a queen. With expensive handbags and designer clothing, Lynn had become sort of a diva herself. All the thrift store clothing that lined her closet three months ago was now replaced with exclusive fashions from Chanel and Dior.

Nina had indeed showed her a life that she could get accustomed to, but she was ready to give it all up. As soon as Brandon left this evening, she had plans on calling her and breaking it off. It was going to be hard because when she wasn't sharing her time with Brandon, she was with Nina but it was something she had to do. Plus, she'd already told Nina that things with her and Brandon were heating up, so she shouldn't be surprised with Lynn's decision to call it quits.

Lynn set the camera up on the TV stand directly across the room from the bed, hiding it behind some old pictures of her and her father when she was younger, so Brandon wouldn't be able to see it. She then pulled out a pair of laced champagne-colored G-string with matching bra and laid it on the bed. She looked up at the clock to check the time. Nearly seven thirty. Brandon should be arriving shortly.

She rushed into the kitchen to take the meat out of the oven and placed it on the counter to cool. She then hurried back to the bathroom to shower and prepare herself for what she knew would be one of the most unforgettable nights of her life.

After finishing her makeup and slipping into the G-string and matching bra, she grabbed the silk bathrobe Nina had bought her and tied the belt around her tiny waist with ease. She then began plaiting her hair in two braids, the way Brandon always liked it.

Just as she was finishing up, there was a knock at the door. Her heart thudded as she took a deep breath and opened the door for the man she loved. As soon as it swung open, Brandon grabbed her by the waist and pushed her inside with a kiss that made goosebumps form all over her body.

Brandon kicked the front door closed with the heel of his Armani loafers and continued to suck the sweet nectar from Lynn's full lips. He began groping her body with his hands, ending up at her round, supple ass. The thought of finally being able to be with her any time he wanted excited him. Getting those divorce papers drawn up was the best thing he'd ever done.

"I missed you too." Lynn pushed him, trying to get him to focus on the romantic dinner she had prepared for him.

Brandon smiled like a schoolboy who'd just had his first kiss. "I'm sorry, baby. I just couldn't help myself. You looked so damn good when you opened that door, I wanted to rip that robe off and eat you for dinner."

He took another look at the robe she had on. It looked like

the one he'd bought Mia last Christmas from Bloomingdale's.

Lynn's pussy moistened at the thought of taking him up on his offer of skipping dinner and going straight for dessert in the bedroom. She got herself under control and poured Brandon a glass of gin on the rocks. She then opened the refrigerator and returned with an unopened bottle of Merlot she'd saved for this special occasion. She popped the top and poured herself a glass.

Brandon gave her a strange look. "Since when did you start drinking Merlot?"

"My girl Nina got me hooked on it." She took a sip from her glass and placed it on the counter.

"I have to meet this Nina of yours. She sounds like an interesting character."

Lynn smiled and returned the bottle back to the refrigerator. She went on to take care of dinner while Brandon made himself comfortable on the couch.

Brandon flipped on the stereo system, and to his delight, Musiq Soulchild's "Halfcrazy" whispered through the speakers. He bobbed his head to the smooth melody as he took off his shoes and joined Lynn at the kitchen counter for what looked like some good eating to him.

He took his fork and knife and cut a nice chunk out of the sirloin steak and stuffed it in his mouth. The savory taste of basil and thyme filled his jaws, and he felt like he was heaven. He kissed Lynn on the cheek as she sat down beside him to eat her dinner.

When they finished up, Lynn cleared the counter and led Brandon back to the candle-lit bedroom, the scent of fresh jasmine in the air.

"Close your eyes," Lynn said as they crossed the threshold. She led him to the side of the bed. She hurried over to turn the recorder on and peeled off the robe she had on over her bra and panty set, revealing her luscious feminine curves and silky smooth skin. "Okay, now you can open them." She smiled seductively.

Brandon looked at the beautiful woman before him and his smile automatically turned upside down. "What are you doing here?" he asked, easing himself off the bed to stand up. He looked across the room at Mia, who was sporting an all-black spandex jumpsuit and dark cat-eyed Gucci sunglasses with blood-red MAC lipstick.

"I think the question is, what the hell are you doing here?" Mia placed her leather-gloved hand on her hip.

"It can't be," Lynn said.

Mia grabbed her face and kissed her fervently in front of Brandon, causing him to get a little stiff one in the pants.

"What are you doing here, Nina?" Lynn pushed her aside and wiped the lipstick off her lips.

"Nina?" Brandon asked in a confused tone. "That's no Nina. That's Mia, my wife!"

"Your wife? It-it can't be," Lynn said, shaking her head.

"Oh, but it is," Mia said. "See, Brandon, me and your little girl toy here have been fooling around." She grinned. "And I must say, she was a hell of a lay." Mia cupped her hand across her mouth as if she was telling a secret and then said, "The girl can eat a pussy better than you. Who would figure?"

Lynn looked over at Brandon and then back at Mia, who were staring each other down like hawks.

It all made sense to Brandon now, the familiar voice on the phone when he was visiting with Lynn, the necklace he'd bought her for Valentine 's Day. Mia had set him up good, but that didn't mean that he wasn't going to leave Lynn.

"So you fucked her a couple of times. Who cares?" Brandon lay back down on the bed and made himself comfortable, his hands behind his head. "The important thing is that I love her and not you."

Mia's face turned bright red, and her eyes grew dark with rage. She snatched the black snakeskin Prada clutch from under her arm and pulled out a black Glock 26. "I care, pussy," she said, waving the gun in his direction. "You think you just gonna get away, for all the stuff you did to me? Well, guess again, Negro, 'cause your ass is gonna pay. And your little hoe-ass girlfriend over here is going to take the blame."

Lynn backed away from Mia.

"Your mother told me you were a nut case."

"My mother? My mother? That crackhead bitch doesn't know what the hell she's talking about half the time. I do what I have to do to survive."

Brandon scrambled to sit up in the bed. He looked over at Lynn and then back over at Mia. "You lied to me too, Mia. Or should I say Tifah. What about your two other husbands? That's right, I know about them."

"What about them? You think I care about those losers? They were just like you, a pretender. They didn't have any real money, so I had to get rid of them and what better way to do that than to make sure they had unexplained accidents and collect off their insurance polices."

Brandon instantly thought about the letter he'd received in the mail about her upping his life insurance policy. When he'd approached her about it, she made it seem as though she was just adding the baby on.

Lynn began to whimper, shielding her naked body with her arms. She couldn't believe she was so naïve about her relationship with Mia. She ought to have known she was up to something when she always asked her how her and Brandon's sex was.

Brandon looked over at Lynn, who leaned helplessly against the closet door, the fear of God in her eyes. "Why don't you leave her out of this? We can settle it ourselves."

"You must be kidding," Mia said, releasing the safety. "You should have thought about that before you stuck your dick in her and that physical therapist at the hospital. That's right, I seen her bouncing up and down on you like a little jackrabbit in heat. I forgave you once in hopes that you would get your shit together, but no, you just had to go fuck up again. And to add insult to injury, you went back to the same bitch that almost cost us our marriage in the first place. You have to pay. Let's not forget you're broke. You're worth more to me dead than alive now anyway."

In the heat of the moment, Brandon charged toward Mia, pushing Lynn down to safety in the process and extending his right arm to grab the gun.

Mia let off three shots back to back, sending stainless steel bullets ripping through his neck, arm, and grazing the side of his temple and lodging itself in the bedroom wall behind him. She stood stunned, yet pleased as Brandon's 200-pound frame hit the ground in a loud thump.

Lynn stood paralyzed in the same spot. She wanted to scream, but nothing would come out.

"Catch." Mia tossed the gun in her direction.

Afraid that if the gun hit the floor, it would go off, Lynn caught it.

"Silly, girl," Mia said, walking toward the door. She knew Lynn didn't have the heart to use it. Plus, her precious Brandon was lying on the ground dying. She exited the apartment and dialed the police as she stepped on the elevator.

"Nine-one-one," the operator said.

"I just heard gunshots down the hall from my apartment. I live in Pennsylvania House. Please come quickly," she said frantically, pressing the button for the lobby. She hung up quickly. She placed her shades back on her face and strutted through the lobby and out the door right past the police as they were pulling up to the curb. Her job was done, and the insurance money was hers. All she had to do was play her part at the funeral and collect.

The policeman barged into the room and found Lynn holding the murder weapon in her hand. "Drop it!" They grabbed her and swung her down to the ground.

"But I didn't do it."

As they placed the cuffs on her, her eyes met Brandon. He looked as though he was still breathing.

"Call an ambulance!" she shouted as they picked her up from the ground and hauled her away. "He's still alive!"

One of the policemen immediately got on the walkie-talkie and summoned an ambulance.

Lynn looked back at Brandon as they escorted her out the bedroom by the arm. She held her head low as she entered the hallway and walked past the crowd of neighbors gathered at the door.

Lynn wheeled Brandon up the narrow aisle toward the front of the courtroom. His eyes stayed glued to the raised platform in front of him where the judge would soon sit. The courtroom was fairly quiet, with only a few people here and there spread out around the room. The jury stand sat vacant, since Mia waived her rights.

It had been eight months since he'd last seen Mia, and he wasn't thrilled to come face to face again with her today. After the cops found the video tape that Lynn planted with Mia confessing to not only plan to kill Brandon, but the death of her other two husbands, they released Lynn and brought Mia back from Mexico to stand trial.

The bullet that hit Brandon in the neck penetrated his spi-nal cord, paralyzing him from the neck down. He felt lucky to be alive, but he was also miserable knowing that he would never be himself again. At times, he wished he'd died that night, but when he thought about his daughter and Lynn, he realized he was still the luckiest man on earth.

He watched as Lynn, now five months pregnant with his second child, a son, took a seat in the courtroom audience.

If it's one thing Brandon learned through this whole thing, it was that money and success meant nothing if you didn't have someone decent to share it with. He was indeed a lucky man. He'd finally married the right woman, and for all the right reasons.

Brandon would always be reminded of how he treated other people. And even though, to some, being confined to a wheelchair was worse than death, for him it was a new begin-ning. He wouldn't be able to run around with his children like he would like to, but just getting to see them on a daily basis would be more than enough.

The bailiff asked everyone to stand when the judge entered through the side door and took his rightful place.

Brandon looked over at Mia. Her skin looked pale and dry, and her hair lay neatly in two cornrows. She reminded him of those chicks from the movie, *Set It Off*. His eyes met hers, and she quickly turned away. He couldn't even remember what attracted him to her in the first place. She was a shallow trick-ster who didn't care who she hurt. But then again that too was Brandon a while back. He said a quick prayer thanking God for allowing him to see the light.

The bailiff interrupted his thoughts once more. "Mr. Brunson, would you please take the stand."

Brandon maneuvered his wheelchair over to the witness stand and waited for further instructions.

"Mr. Brunson, do you swear to tell the truth, the whole truth, and nothing but the truth, so help you God?" he said, placing the Bible in front of him.

"I do."

ORDER FORM
URBAN BOOKS, LLC
78 E. Industry Ct
Deer Park, NY 11729


Name:(please print):_____

Address:        _____

City/State:      _____

Zip:            _____

| QTY | TITLES | PRICE |
|---|---|---|
| | 16 ½ On The Block | $14.95 |
| | 16 On The Block | $14.95 |
| | Betrayal | $14.95 |
| | Both Sides Of The Fence | $14.95 |
| | Cheesecake And Teardrops | $14.95 |
| | Denim Diaries | $14.95 |
| | Happily Ever Now | $14.95 |
| | Hell Has No Fury | $14.95 |
| | If It Isn't love | $14.95 |
| | Last Breath | $14.95 |
| | Loving Dasia | $14.95 |
| | Say It Ain't So | $14.95 |

Shipping and Handling - add $3.50 for 1st book then $1.75 for each additional book.
Please send a check payable to:
    **Urban Books, LLC**
Please allow 4 - 6 weeks for delivery

## ORDER FORM
## URBAN BOOKS, LLC
78 E. Industry Ct
Deer Park, NY 11729

Name:(please print):_____ _____

Address:        _____

City/State:     _____

Zip:            _____

| QTY | TITLES | PRICE |
|-----|--------|-------|
| | The Cartel | $14.95 |
| | The Cartel#2 | $14.95 |
| | The Dopeman's Wife | $14.95 |
| | The Prada Plan | $14.95 |
| | Gunz And Roses | $14.95 |
| | Snow White | $14.95 |
| | A Pimp's Life | $14.95 |
| | Hush | $14.95 |
| | Little Black Girl Lost 1 | $14.95 |
| | Little Black Girl Lost 2 | $14.95 |
| | Little Black Girl Lost 3 | $14.95 |
| | Little Black Girl Lost 4 | $14.95 |

Shipping and Handling - add $3.50 for 1st book then $1.75 for each additional book.
Please send a check payable to:
**Urban Books, LLC**
Please allow 4 - 6 weeks for delivery